# TIME SHARING

# TIME SHARING

Richard Krawiec

VIKING
Viking Penguin Inc., 40 West 23rd Street,
New York, New York 10010, U.S.A.
Penguin Books Ltd, Harmondsworth, Middlesex, England
Penguin Books Australia Ltd, Ringwood, Victoria, Australia
Penguin Books Canada Limited, 2801 John Street,
Markham, Ontario, Canada L3R 1B4
Penguin Books (N.Z.) Ltd, 182–190 Wairau Road,
Auckland 10, New Zealand



First published in 1986 by Viking Penguin Inc.
Published simultaneously in Canada

LIBRARY OF CONGRESS CATALOGING IN PUBLICATION DATA
Krawiec, Richard.
Time sharing.
I. Title.
PS3561.R33T5 1986 813′.54 85-40563
ISBN 0-670-80944-6

A portion of this book first appeared,
in slightly different form, in *Antro 14*.



Printed in the United States of America by
R.R. Donnelley & Sons Company, Harrisonburg, Virginia
Set in Fairfield

# DEDICATION

Special thanks to Howard Morhaim, for making it seem easy, and Pat Mulcahy, for not letting me take it easy; to Charles Boyer and Barry Lane, two fine writers and critics who gave unselfishly of their time; and, of course, to Hank, Lorraine, Mary, my family, friends, teachers, Chana—the best Middle Eastern dancer in Boston—and God.

This book is dedicated to the memories of Barry, Bobby, Charley, Eddie, Jan, Ricky, Zip, and especially Karen, who believed in me when I needed it.

# TIME SHARING

# CHAPTER

# —1—

Artie was low on cash. All he had was a pocketful of change from the cigarette machine he'd broken into, and the $5 he got when he pawned Denny's Marine Corps lighter. But he knew the Sin City Strapper was wrestling that night, so he hustled his ass down to the Wrangler Club early and grabbed a front-row table. If he didn't get to the club an hour before the show he'd be stuck in the back and would have to spend the night hopping up to see over other guys' heads. Everyone would be yelling at him the whole time to sit down. Maybe they wouldn't even yell, just move him. It wasn't that he was afraid. No, he wouldn't let himself think that. He just didn't want any trouble. That was it. He was a man who liked the peaceful things. Sensitive.

He ordered a mug from the waitress and pulled a handful of change from the pocket of his dungarees. He piled what he needed on the black plastic tabletop. The table was no bigger than a TV tray and he liked that. When he put his arms down the sides and angled his hands at the wrists he could almost make his fingers touch across the front.

"Seventy-five cents," the waitress said, flopping a napkin onto the table and banging a heavy faceted mug atop it. Beer sloshed over the rim and soaked the napkin.

"Hey, easy with the gold, sweetheart," Artie said. He put his hands around the glass to calm the beer.

"Seventy-five cents, Artie."

"You know me?" He ran his hands forward over his face. When he smiled his lips pulled straight back, like a rodent's. "Yeah, I'm sure I remember you now," he said.

"You don't know me, pal." She rubbed a finger across a cold sore at the corner of her mouth; then she saw the dimes and nickels stacked on the table. She scooped up the pile and dropped his money, one coin at a time, into a highball glass on the cork-surfaced tray she balanced on one hip. "You owe me a nickle," she said, wiggling her fingers at him.

He counted five pennies into her hand. "Don't know you? Are you kidding? You think I could forget a sweetheart like you? No way, darling." He smoothed a hand over his T-shirt, which was black with a white tuxedo front silk-screened on it. He tried to figure where she might hang out, so he could come up with something that sounded possible. She was pretty hard-looking; he'd be safe saying just about anything.

She set her free hand on her other hip and said, "Look, pal, you don't know me from Adam. This is the first time I got stuck with this station, okay? But everybody in here knows you."

"Of course, that's it," he said. He held his hands out in a broad, open gesture. "Everybody knows Artie." He leaned back and rocked on his chair legs. "You caught my eye when I was in here before. You're the kind of girl nobody can forget. Even if they never met you."

"Yeah," she said, "and you're the jerk comes in every Tuesday, nurses one beer for three hours, and then don't leave a dime. You just sit there with your tongue washing the floor. This is a bar, not a goddamned hotel. Some of us got to work for a living." She checked the other customers and started to move off, sliding between Artie's table and the one beside it. The tables were packed so tight she had to turn sideways to squeeze through.

He reached up to grab her arm but stopped when she swung her head back and bared her clenched teeth at him. He pointed his finger like it was a gun, aiming right between her eyes. But his hand shook, and he had to wet his lips and swallow before he could speak. "You're in a lot of trouble, sister. I'm a personal friend of the owner."

"Stow it," she told him. With her back to him, she called out over her shoulder, "You ain't a personal friend of nobody."

He slapped his right hand on the table and twisted around to face the sunken pit where the girls wrestled. A thick-bodied, bearded man wearing dungarees, a leather vest, and a work shirt with the name *Randy* on the pocket dragged a greasy 55-gallon rubbish barrel to the pit. His sleeves were rolled up and there were matching dragon tattoos on his forearms. He tipped the barrel forward, spilling out a quivering slush of red. The Jell-O sparkled under the spotlights, broken dots of white moving like pulses.

Artie tapped his fingers on the table. He'd like to see the waitress in that pit, he thought. He wanted to go at his beer, but he knew if he took that first taste it'd be bottoms up, and they wouldn't let you sit around in here if your glass was empty. It was one of those joints. He couldn't see drinking at their prices, not when he could get a six-pack for what they'd charge him for two. So he sat, looking at his thumbs, waiting for something to happen. He wondered if he should drop in to see his mother. Get himself a free meal. He was thinking it over when a sudden commotion sounded at the entrance. People stomped their feet and started talking louder. Artie perked up. He whistled the melody line of "When the Saints Come Marching In" and looked over his right shoulder to the front door.

The Saints entered in a pack, led by Eric, a big blond who reminded Artie of a Viking. They came in rowdy, hooting and yelling, banging on tables. They besieged the place like an occupation force, the group opening space between themselves, spreading out, looking for trouble spots. They sauntered and swaggered through the club and finally drew back together at their usual spot, the area across from Artie's seat. They filled the front row of tables on the raised platform on that side of the pit, then ignored the next four rows and slumped against the wall.

It seemed like everyone had been waiting for them. The place was suddenly full and raucous. Artie put two fingers in his mouth and gave a cutting whistle, then yipped like a dog.

"Strap-per Strap-per Strap-per," the Saints chanted. Everyone joined in, clapping and stomping their feet in time. The Strapper belonged to Eric. She was only seventeen, a big girl whose flesh just rolled out of her leotard. Nobody cared about that, though, because she wasn't afraid to pull her top down. She always made sure she got her opponent's top down, too; she even made a valiant effort at the bottoms.

"People are primed," Artie said to the person at the table to his left. It appeared to be a woman because of the way her dark hair curled to her shoulders. But when she turned to Artie her face was flat, almost featureless. "Yes," the person said, in a voice that seemed to be in between sexes.

Artie shook it off and looked away. He listened to the whistles and screams flying through the bar. A heavy growl, like a roomful of pit terriers eager to get on with the bloodletting, vibrated the air. The whole place was shaking.

From nowhere the Sin City Strapper appeared, strutting through the foglike smoke that had settled heavy in the pit. She was smiling and squeezing her breasts, shaking them at the Saints, who tossed things in her direction. Plastic cups. Rubbers. A hot dog, which Sin City put in her mouth and sucked, then passed to the woman who worked the bar. The bartender dropped it in the rubbish.

An older rummy, sitting at a front table at the end, got hit in the face with a cup of beer. The liquid splashed upward in an amber spurt that caught a few flashes of white from the spotlights before it fell into the pit. The rummy stood up, but before he could get anywhere the Saints were on him. All Artie could see were leather jackets and arms flailing; a pool cue; knees coming up and boots stomping down. There was a brief opening in a few of the front-row seats as people hurried to get away from there. When the Saints pulled back, bodies surged for the empty seats. A scuffle broke out between a dude in a cardigan sweater and a spade wearing a cowboy hat, but Randy broke it up by decking the kid in the sweater with one punch to the face. "Way to go, Randy," Artie called, but no one heard him. The spade smiled and rocked back onto the rear legs of his chair, his hat balanced on his knee. The Saints looked around with bright eyes, pleased with the way things were going.

"All right all right *all right!*" Bobby Dame yelled through the microphone on the bar. Bobby refereed all the matches. He was a big-bellied energetic man who always wore a white T-shirt, green gym shorts, and broken-down, laceless, ankle-high Keds. "Son . . . Son? . . . *Sin,* yeah, Sin City Strapper," he called, and the screaming rattled the glasses in the rack above the bar. The Strapper shook herself all over, then paused and turned slowly, like a beauty contestant. "Okay, that's enough, you guys, that's enough, now quiet down. Quiet down. *Shut up,* I said," Bobby hollered. "Come on now, you people get a hold of your meat. I got something important to announce. Give me a break." The noise subsided and Bobby looked around, his eyes sly and promising. He pulled at his crotch. Making his voice sound like Ed McMahon's, he said, "Tonight, we have a *first-time* wrestler." He paused while laughs and hoots filled the place. Then he held up his hand for silence. "So let me introduce to you . . . the Massacre Mama!"

When she heard the name she didn't remember at first that he meant her. She was sitting on the toilet in the ladies' room because her legs were shaky and she held in her mind an image of herself trying to walk, but unable to because her legs would snap into splintered pieces and she'd collapse to the floor.

Maybe it wouldn't have been so bad if they had a dressing room at least. But she'd had to change in the dirty stall, and in the middle some girl started banging on the door, not saying a word, just wanting to get in. When Jolene hurried out, whispering "Excuse me" and "I'm sorry," trying to smile an apology, she was confronted with a face of stark, unfocused want. A wasted face, beyond age, sucking in on itself. The girl said nothing, just pushed Jolene aside with a fist that clutched a short strand of rope. Jolene watched as the door to the stall clanked shut and the bolt lock snapped into place.

She looked at the girl's legs where they showed at the bottom of the door. She sat down without slipping off her pants and placed an oversized brown cloth bag between her leather ankle boots. Rummaging through it, she found, then dropped, a blackened tablespoon. It clattered on the cement floor and the girl's hand pounced on it like a wrestler seeking a three-count pin. In one motion hand and spoon disappeared upward.

"Do you wrestle too?" Jolene asked the door. The only reply was a soft moan. Jolene waited a long time for the girl to come out. As the door swung open Jolene asked, "Can you give me any pointers?"

The bones seemed to have dissolved beneath the girl's skin, and her mouth was set in a grin that floated from side to side on her face. It was then that the big-bellied man, Bobby, had entered the ladies' room. He pushed the girl outside and asked Jolene what name she was using. He laughed when she told him her own.

"How bad do you want to win?" he asked. He reached a hand down the front of his shorts and backed her toward the toilet. Excitement pulsed from him in surges.

"I don't care if I win or lose. I just want my twenty-five dollars." She started to tell him about her baby, trying to explain to him that she was a mother, trying to make a few bucks. Bobby laughed at her and she almost got mad. "I'll do the best I can. I don't need any help," she told him.

His mood switched. He took on the aspect of a boy who'd just been scolded. Walking backward toward the door, he told her, "You can be the Massacre Mama." He had a look on his face, like he knew some dangerous private joke. She didn't know that he was naming her. She thought he was just talking, putting her down like men always did.

"Massacre Mama, come on down," the voice called out again. It was tinny from the microphone but contained a rough urgency that cut through the savage garble of voices and laughter that seemed to exist out there as a presence in itself. Jolene realized he was calling for her.

He yelled once more and she opened the bathroom door and looked through the club, packed so tight there didn't appear to be an aisle for her to walk down. She was behind the bulk of them, at the back of the place, and something about their heads and shoulders, the bobbing shrugs and rolls of motion, reminded her of something she'd seen on television a long time ago: carrion beetles, the kind that swarmed over dead carcasses and picked them clean.

She stepped out and told herself, "Our Father who art in heaven," thinking she might as well pray as do anything. There was silence, then laughter, and she couldn't remember the rest. Something about a halo? She strode forward, trying to keep her mind blank and her eyes on the spotlighted pit full of red, peaked waves of Jell-O that reminded her of frozen flames. The pit was the only place she could be apart from them all, left alone except for the other girl, who stood watching Jolene wedge her way through the crowd, the girl with her hands on her hips and a sneer slicing open her face. Jolene looked at her and thought, She's only a kid. The realization seemed to connect them somehow, and Jolene felt that they were exalted above the grunting mass.

But the crowd forced its way back onto her immediately. She tried not to listen as the voices roared about "tits" and "ass" and "cunt." Fingers slid over her thighs, between her legs. She was pinched and slapped from behind, but she wouldn't look back. Hands reached up for her breasts and she pushed them aside with her arms. She kept apologizing, as if it were her fault. And then, oh God, as she turned sideways to slip between two tables, she felt the hot wet slurp of what could only be someone's tongue run up the back of her leg. Teeth nipped her ass. Laughter peppered out behind her, and she moved her legs in big extended strides that caused her to slam and bump against the tables. She wondered how long she could function like this, without thinking.

Then she was at the pit. "It's cold," she told Bobby after she'd dipped her foot in, as if testing water.

"Get your big lazy ass in here." Grabbing her wrists, he pulled her forward so that she stumbled onto her hands and knees. The coldness of the Jell-O hit her with the shock of a sudden judgment. The voices took on a rounded, aggressive quality, like the calls of a pack of dogs in heat, and she hung her head and tried to block out all the noise. She repeated the single truth that might get her through the next nine minutes: I am a mother. And then the second truth revealed itself, following the first like the damage that comes after an explosion: If I had to I would do much worse.

Everything seemed to be pointing to a great show, Artie thought. It had been so funny: the way she'd poked her head out of the bathroom, smiling shyly; the careful way she'd stepped out, as if she were afraid of disturbing someone. For a split second there'd been no sound as everyone looked at her long, gangly body. Then it was as if everyone noticed for the first time that she was wearing a V-necked Danskin, the easiest thing in the world for Sin City to pull down. There'd been a sudden increased hum of anticipation, followed by a laughing buzz that started at the tables near her and rippled back through the crowd toward ringside; then she must've realized it too, because she blessed herself. The crowd had exploded.

As she moved toward the pit, everyone kept calling things to her, fooling around and reaching out. She pushed everyone's hands aside, but the way she'd kept her face polite, and nodded apologies, it seemed as though she understood that it was all for laughs. Then when she dipped her foot into the pit and Bobby pulled her forward . . . well, that was too much.

Seeing her up close now, Artie was worried and confused. She didn't seem too excited. He examined her as if checking over a racehorse. Her hair was bleached, and the way it was cut, so close to her scalp, it made her face look drawn and mulelike. Even kneeling, she looked tall. She had strong thighs, and a puffy belly that made him wonder if she'd had a kid. People continued calling things to her, sexual things, commenting, challenging, joking. The mood of the crowd was festive, and Artie was disappointed that she didn't seem to be enjoying it at all. She sat in the corner with her head low, breathing hard. He found himself feeling sorry for her; it was obvious she didn't know what she was getting into. But he didn't want to think about that. It might spoil his fun.

Bobby Dame gave the rules, then stepped between the girls and wiped his mouth with the back of his hand. Grabbing each by one shoulder, he positioned them so that they knelt in the center of the pit, facing each other. He rubbed his hands along their backs. Someone yelled, "Dame's got a boner." He laughed and called out, to nobody in particular, "You wish you could still get one." Everyone laughed some more. Then he blew the whistle and hopped backward. The Massacre Mama smiled and held out her hand for a shake and the crowd just howled. Sin City whipped a clot of Jell-O right into her face; it splattered all over.

Artie leaned across the table until his head was nearly in the ring. It seemed he could taste the sweat, a thick, salty, coppery flavor. The Massacre was on the defensive, sliding out of grips and moving away, and her scent grew even stronger. Early on, when she accidentally pulled down the Strapper's top, the Massacre relaxed her guard and moved quickly to help the Strapper cover up. She didn't seem to understand why everyone thought that was funny. She bowed her head to the Strapper and said, "I'm really sorry." What a big mistake. The Strapper pushed her down onto her stomach and pinned her on a quick count, Dame yelling "onetwothree" before his hand descended once. The Massacre looked hurt and betrayed. She tried to protest, said something about "time out," and the laughter boomed so loudly that she shrunk down and looked around, her face white, her eyes large and distinct.

Everyone knew that was it. There were two more rounds to go, but it was all over. The technical part was done. Now the Strapper could get to the important stuff. The hooting started in once more, louder than ever. The crowd revved up like a racing engine. Heads shifted from side to side to get a better view.

Sin City pulled up the bottom of Massacre's body suit to show her fleshy cheeks, and when her opponent moved to cover them, she pulled down the top of the Massacre's Danskin to expose her breasts. Every time the Massacre went to cover up one part, the Strapper was busy opening up another. She's a real artist, that Strapper, Artie thought, a regular ballerina of the Jell-O pit.

The Massacre Mama kept getting madder and more upset. Her head pointed lower and lower. Her eyes flashed all over the place. But Sin City wouldn't let up. The boys went insane. A chant roared through the joint—*tit tit tit tit tit*—and everyone was laughing and whistling so hard Artie could hardly hear himself scream.

The rounds blended together—Bobby never kept track of time if people were having fun—and after about twenty minutes Sin City just tore Massacre's top clean down to her navel. The whole crowd surged forward to get a look. The thick smoke seemed to lift from the pit and the Massacre was clearly visible, sagging on her knees and trying not to cry. It made everyone even more excited. She held up the front of her Danskin halfheartedly. There were bits of Jell-O smeared all over her skin, catching the light and shining off in pinpoints of white. Her hair was so wet and matted it looked to be a hazy brown color; the short strands clumped together and skewed out at odd angles. She peered up at all the faces, crowding in over the tables around the ring, and her features tightened. Bobby Dame moved quickly, shoving several guys back to keep them from climbing into the pit.

Artie shook his head. The Massacre was in the wrong place, he thought. But she was doing the best she could. It was apparent she didn't know anybody there, and it didn't look like she'd brought any friends with her. He rubbed his neck and squinted at her. Maybe she was going to need someone to talk to afterward, he thought. After she got paid. He looked at the spotlights shining down from the ceiling and imagined himself striding into the pit, silencing the joint with a slice of his hand, then lifting her out of there: Now don't worry about what you owe me, darling, this one's on me. Of course they'd both know the truth—that she'd owe him forever.

There was a loud, gleeful rumble and he saw that the Strapper had yanked the Massacre's top down even lower, exposing a tattoo of a butterfly on her abdomen. The crowd hushed, as if to catch a breath, and then the place went wild. Massacre yelled, "Just cut that shit out!" before she took a swinging punch at the Strapper. A scared little-girl look snapped onto the Strapper's face. The heads around the pit pulled back a bit. A low "Oooooh" exhaled through the club.

Bobby Dame waggled his finger at the Massacre. "Hey, wrestle fair. This ain't no serious fighting. It's just for a few yuks." Everyone applauded.

Sin City looked around the place and smiled. She pulled her own top down and just let it all hang out.

"Oh, I can't watch this," Bobby said, putting his hands over his eyes with his fingers spread wide open.

The Strapper knelt proud, turning so everyone could get their eyes full. She seemed to be taking her mood from the crowd. When she had finished giving views all around, she stood stock-still. "Think you're too good?" she screamed, then slid forward on her knees and tore the Massacre's top down one last time. Bobby blew the whistle. The Strapper stood up and he held her hand aloft.

The Massacre slumped down, face to the pit, covering up. She took in hard, ragged breaths, pinched her nose with one hand, and fixed her Danskin. She tilted her head up, her mouth set, her eyes not looking at anyone. The crowd was already celebrating.

Artie was enveloped in the good feeling too, but when he looked down at the Massacre Mama he knew just what was up. She was ready to need somebody, and she'd probably pay whatever was necessary for a little kindness.

The bartender rang the bell signaling the official end of the match. Bobby Dame bent over and whipped down his gym shorts and shot them all a moon. Crazy bastard, Artie thought, and added his laugh to the others tumbling through the Wrangler like a landslide. He lifted his beer. It was flat and warm but he drained it in one long series of gulps. He hated to split without seeing the rest of the show—there were five more matches—but he had a feeling the Massacre wasn't going to hang around. He'd bet on it. Sometimes, he told himself as he stood up and flipped a dime onto the tabletop, you just gotta go for it.

# CHAPTER
# —2—

It was cold outside and raw from the sleet that had hit the ground earlier that night. As he started down the street, Artie noticed how the snow from the previous month's storm still filled the gutters, but it was covered over with a brown-gray layer of dirt so you couldn't tell it was snow unless you knew it was there to begin with. All down the street soft-edged lines of red, yellow, and white, reflections of the store signs, streetlamps, and car headlights, wavered on the wet asphalt. The lines of color looked solid, but as he stared he noticed the holes and ridges in the tar pimpling through the colors, like the black dots on an unfocused television screen. He thought it would be nice if he could take those colors and cover up the white walls of his room. He thought of it as his room, even though he shared it with Denny.

A couple strolled toward him on the sidewalk. They were indifferently dressed, neither stylish nor poor, and Artie stepped out of their way. He rubbed his hands forward over his face, then brisked them together, palm to palm, and blew on them. Once they were past him, Artie checked them out closer. He noted the woman's small purse, the thin, easily snapped strap by which it hung off her shoulder. He had better things to try for tonight, he thought; anyways, the guy looked like a runner. Artie clicked out rapid bursts on the sidewalk with the taps on the bottoms of his high-heeled dagger-toed black boots. The quick taps were grouped like distress signals.

Brick apartment buildings sagged against each other up and down the street. All the windows were closed, but fast, heavy music still thumped a sound track into the night. Artie wished he had a radio or something. Because music . . . well, that was something that could save you from yourself. A car horn honked and a siren screeched somewhere in the distance. It was a nice sound tonight, since he didn't have to worry about it being for him.

The windowless door behind him rattled open, and by the time he had turned the Massacre Mama was already past him and tearing off up the sidewalk. She was moving so fast he was out of breath just trying to catch up with her.

"Hey, Massacre," he made the word sound as tender as he could. She was bigger than she looked in the pit, a long, lanky woman much taller than himself. The hell with that, he thought.

"Leave me alone, you creep," she said. She wore a blue cloth coat that ran just past her knees. It was ripped under one armpit. Her hands stayed deep in her pockets and he wondered, Gun? He was careful not to touch her.

"I will," he said. "I ain't here to bother you. I swear I never been in there before. I just wanted to tell you it wasn't right, what they did to you. It was disgusting." He had to stop walking to think about what he should say next. His jacket, an old green bomber-pilot style with nubby yellow material on the inside, was unzipped halfway. He wanted to show off his shirt and the curls of black hair creeping out over the collar. But it was just so damn cold he had no choice. He pulled the zipper tight to his neck, then hurried to catch up with her again. As he ran he thought about how women didn't appreciate none of the display men made for them.

"I respect you for what you tried to do." He stopped in front of her, then fell in by her side as she kept on walking. "Bring a little class to that joint. Just like an artist. I ain't never seen nobody do that before." He recalled the swinging punch she took at the Strapper and nodded appreciatively.

"I thought you never *been* there before."

He put his arms out in protest and tried to make his face look innocent. His teeth showed black and yellow. "Hell, what can I say? I just wanted to meet a lady like you. Someone with real class. Someone with pride in themselves. I know, I know—you don't have to say nothing. It's crazy. What could you see in a guy like me? But hell . . . even just a hello-goodbye would be a memory I would treasure forever."

She gave him a long look, pulling her head back and tilting it from side to side, as if she were looking at a child's drawing and trying to figure out what it was supposed to be and which way to hold it.

He said, "I'll just see you to the corner and be on my way. No hassles."

She didn't say anything, but she walked slower, and when he offered her a Camel she let him light it for her, her hand just touching his as they both cupped the match.

"A lady like you. What do they know?"

"Thanks. I appreciate the kindness."

They passed a Chinese restaurant; in the light cast by the glaring sign the sidewalk glowed red and gold; the colors caught them and rolled over their faces in twisted stripes.

"But that gets me so mad," she said. "When I think about what she done to me. And her just a kid. I . . . Oooooh. Oooooh, why'd she have to do that? Why'd she have to go and degrade me like that?"

"Forget it. You couldn't see nothing anyways," he said. "'Course, I didn't look." They were in front of a bar with stained-glass windows and plants hanging from the ceiling over the tables. Two men in suits stood up against the glass. They spoke to each other, then looked at Artie, laughing, and raised their drinks to him. He looked away.

"Really? You couldn't see?" she asked.

"Nah. It was too dark." He smiled at her. "It all looked like Jell-O anyways."

She snapped her head to look at him and stopped moving. He glanced over to see the men still watching them.

"Come on now," he said. "I'm just trying to make a joke. Don't go getting heated up on me." As he held his hands above his shoulders and walked forward, he noticed a cop idling on the corner across the street, in front of a discount drugstore. Artie smoothed his hands down his jacket and pants, patted his pockets. Just to be sure he wasn't carrying anything hot. She pulled up and matched her stride to his.

They walked on in silence and he decided to try a different tactic. He dragged on his cigarette without using his hands to hold it. She didn't take any notice though, just dawdled along with her head half down like she was thinking. So maybe he'd try a French inhale, show her how worldly he was. He jutted his chin forward and puffed rapidly, walking fast to stay just ahead of her so she could get a clear view. When she looked up at him he stopped and let the smoke roll out of his mouth, then took it in his nostrils. "I learned that in Paris."

The Massacre took a hard suck on her cigarette, burning up the last third of it, and threw the butt on the sidewalk. "I learned that in Boston." Artie had to stop himself from moving to pick it up.

He wasn't sure what to do next. He could tell her he thought he was falling in love with her. Sometimes that worked, but usually it was better to wait a day or two, and for some reason it worked better with fat women. Or maybe he should tell her his mother had just died. Girls had a soft spot for that kind of thing.

They came to a Dunkin' Donuts and she paused to eye the display case. Inside, right up against the glass door, was a drunk with a beard like a foamy Brillo pad and a slash on his nose oozing pus. He became animated, stomping one foot and contorting his arms as if performing a ritual dance. He opened and closed his mouth like a fish. Artie looked past him.

At stools halfway down, on the curve of the counter, two spades with their hair in Rasta curls sat before large glasses of Pepsi. Back at the far end, a pair of longhairs in leather jackets banged their hands on the counter and sang a song to each other, squinting their eyes and shaking their heads to emphasize the lyrics. It was one of those setups that could go either way, Artie thought. They'd all leave you alone, or someone might edge into trouble.

He looked at the Massacre and decided she was big enough to take care of herself.

"Check out that old biddy," Artie said. He pointed through the window at the white-haired waitress, who leaned against the metal counter in front of the coffee machine. She blew cigarette smoke straight down at the floor and picked at her hangnails with her teeth. Artie laughed, trying to get the Massacre to go along with his fun. "Imagine if that was your mother," he said.

"It could be worse," she said quietly. She looked at the racks of tawny donuts, some iced, some plain, all old and cool. To Artie she seemed to be staring less at the donuts than at her own reflection.

He said, "Let me get you a cup of coffee, sweetheart."

She shook her head and mumbled, "I don't know about that."

"Ah, come on, it's just coffee. There's lights. There's people around. What do you think, I'm going to try to slap the make on you in Dunkin' Donuts? Give me credit for a little more class than that." He looked into the store. "You don't have to worry about them in there. I used to be a boxer in the service." He looked over at her, but when she looked back he avoided her eyes. He pressed his hand to the window between their reflections. "You're with me. What could be safer?" His breath fogged the glass.

"Well, maybe just one cup." She moved over to the door and stood there, her hands in her coat pockets; he wondered what she was waiting for. Finally she nodded at the door.

"Sorry, I thought you were one of them liberated ones." Leave it to women to make it complicated, he thought. "I didn't want to offend you." When he pulled the door open for her the drunk stumbled out, waving his arms in circles.

"My name's Jolene Handy," she told Artie as she stepped into the vestibule.

"You can call me Artie," he said, standing on his toes so that his mouth was level with the base of her neck.

They took the first two stools, and before he had spun around three times, she had begun to go to town. All he could do was watch. She ate two eclairs, a French cruller, a jelly donut, and a bismarck. She just packed it in. He wondered for a second if Lent was starting, but then he got too nervous to think about it. He touched the crumpled bill in his pocket.

When she mentioned she'd like to get one little something to go he felt like walking out, cutting his losses. But he was in too deep. He didn't want to start hitting on her for money just yet. Though he could bet the Wrangler had already paid her.

"I just want to take one little donut home, but it's not for me," she said. "It's for Dandy."

"Who?"

"My boy. That's why I said I'd wrestle at the Wrangler. I want us to be something better than we are, and there ain't many respectable ways left for a girl to make some money. I don't want to do nothing like massage."

"Oh no, 'course not, you save your massaging for the man who loves you." Artie bent forward and turned his face toward her.

She lowered her head to her coffee cup and sipped. "I got to take care of my kid."

"Dandy," he said. He eased back and twirled around once on his stool. "Dandy Handy."

"That's right."

He shook his head. Don't that beat all, he thought. "You know, I always believed it was those little things, like your name, things outside of you, that kind of set how you end up in life. Like me—Artie. Arturo, really. See, my old lady named me after her brother, who used to sing opera before he went and died from love."

"How can you die from love?" she asked. "I can see where someone who loves you might kill you. But that ain't dying. That's being murdered. If you're going to talk to me, talk the truth." She ran her hand over the pile of wax papers the donuts had come on. She had stacked the papers neatly, then flattened them as best she could. She picked up the stack now and folded the papers into her coat pocket.

"Ah, truth, lies, stories; it's all just words," Artie said. He watched her put the wax papers in her pocket, then he pulled a wad of napkins from the metal dispenser and put them in his coat pocket. "Now just hush up and I'll tell you." He put a faraway look in his eyes, shook his head as if remembering pain; he sighed, then began.

"Remember them Coppertone billboards where this mutt is pulling down this little girl's bathing suit and you can see how dark her tan is by how white her ass is? Excuse my French, but you know what I mean. We're two mature adults, we can talk about this stuff, right?"

She nodded.

"Good. Well, my uncle was in love with that little girl's ass. He used to talk about it all the time, comparing the girls in the neighborhood to it, that sort of stuff. He yapped so much even I got sick of it. But that wasn't bad enough. He had to stand on the corner looking up at the billboard and sing to it. In Italian. Christ, I'm telling you." From the corner of his eye Artie saw the spades lean toward each other and whisper. He knew they had to be talking about him. When they stood up he put his palms to the counter and waited. He figured he could jump over it and maybe grab a pot of hot coffee to throw on them. They strutted slowly toward him and Artie tensed his neck and arms. But they just walked on, out the door, without even glancing back.

"Is that it?" Jolene asked. She had her chin in her hand, propped up by her arm on the counter.

"Just hold your horses, I'm getting to the best part," he told her, smiling. "Anyways, this building that the billboard was on was the lamp factory. It was right at the end of the projects, and Miss Coppertone there was right at the top of the building. About—um, eight stories up, overlooking the expressway. So one day my uncle gets shit-faced on his lunch break. I mean, the guy was plowed. Seems they were all sitting around in the factory lunchroom doing some nips. So my uncle laid down some cash, saying he could climb up there and plant a wet one on those cheeks. Jimmy Three Fingers held all the bets—he was always the guy for handling money—and he was going to snap a picture of the whole thing. For proof. So they go up in the elevator, one guy on each floor watching out for the foremen, and they make it to the roof no problem. So Uncle Arturo starts in to climbing."

He watched Jolene finish chewing what was in her mouth and swallow it. When he looked down he realized she had taken a bite from his plain donut. Not just a bite, a gobble. It's an investment, he told himself, but he still felt kind of mad. He looked around. The longhairs had left. The waitress was at the far end of the counter, wiping it down with a cloth that had turned gray from use. Jolene smiled at him and stuffed the other half of his donut into her mouth. She nodded to him to go on, like she was interested, as she chewed the donut from cheek to cheek.

He didn't feel like telling her the story anymore, and he worked hard to control his anger. It bothered him too, not wanting to tell the story, because he had figured out a whole scene with blood and everything, for effect.

"What happened?" she said, the sounds round and distorted as they traveled past the lumps of donut still in her mouth.

"What's there to say?" He stared at her. "He fell onto the highway and a couple of cars, maybe a trailer truck, ran him over before the traffic slowed and someone stopped to see what the problem was."

She sat for a second, looking sideways at him, letting it settle in; then she gasped. "My God, Artie! That's horrible. Did you see it?"

That softened him enough to get him back into it a little. He sighed and shook his head. "Yeah, I was right there the whole time, watching with them from the roof. I was the only one up there. They always thought I was important enough, and smart enough, to be in on all the grown-up things."

He started to smile but caught himself quickly and pressed his lips together.

"But looking down at my uncle, him having the same name—man, it was like looking down at me. Like I was the one that was the screwed-up mess. So that kind of put a damper on Arturo for me, you know? That's why I call myself Artie. And all these years, I been kind of careful with women, saving myself for that lucky one, because when I find that one I truly love, I know—I know I would die for her too."

They both looked at the white Formica counter as if the gold flecks scattered throughout it were messages from the future, only needing to be put together right.

After a time Artie turned to Jolene with a laugh. "Why'd you go and name that boy Dandy? Why couldn't you name him something normal?" He gulped from his coffee cup and banged it on the counter for the waitress to refill.

"What are you bringing that up again for?" She watched the waitress fill their cups and said, "Thank you."

The woman nodded her head without looking at them.

"Do you have kids?" Jolene asked; the waitress gave her a look of angry confusion, then turned away without answering.

"I was just thinking," Artie said. "Bert Handy. Now that sounds like something a boy could grow into. Bert Handy—garage mechanic."

"I don't see nothing wrong in my boy's name."

"Your name, it . . . it's . . . it sets things. It's like magic, you know?"

"Believe me, I know." She opened her mouth to say something else but looked at Artie and changed her mind.

"What the hell—Dandy Handy's Donuts? I don't think so." He leaned forward and tilted his face to look up into hers. "Just think, if you had named him something like Awful. Awful Handy. Why, the kid could grow up to be a Mr. Fixit." She wouldn't look at him, and he wondered if he had said something wrong. "Are you upset? Don't worry about it. It's not your fault. This is something men think about. Women, they think about things like . . . I don't know what."

"My boy's name was good enough for Henry."

"Who?"

"Dandy's daddy."

"Henry Handy?" Artie asked. He twirled in his seat and called out "Wheeee!" He grabbed the counter to stop himself. "Well, that about says it all." He wondered why she ever let someone named that lie down with her. She must never have been too choosy, he thought. He was beginning to like his chances. Best part of it, she was kind of nice to be with too. She listened to him. If only she'd stop eating.

He reached over and covered her larger hand with his. She tried to pull away but he pulled it to the counter. She yanked it away a second time and he pulled it back again. He held it there, even as she tried to slide it away, and he said, "Hey now. Hey now. Whoa, gal. Now listen. I'm just kidding. I've always been a joker. Life-of-the-party Artie, that's me. You'll see. I'm a poet and I don't know it. I'm a good time." He looked at her face and tried to keep straight everything he had told her so far. "Look, it don't matter none to me what his name is, or who you've been with. We all get dirty and we all take baths, right? It's true. Would I lie to you? Besides, I love kids."

She sat back and stared at him for a while. Just when he thought he'd have to give in and turn away her eyes widened and her face softened up into a smile. "If you can look me in the eye like that—" She wiped her mouth with the sleeve of her coat, then touched him on the arm. She turned to the waitress and called, "I'll have a filled donut. And two to go."

They stepped into the street, checking for traffic as they moved. A set of headlights shone, blinding them, as a car took a right turn onto the street from the alley to their left. Artie grabbed Jolene's elbow to get her to dash out of the way with him. "Slow down," she yelled at the car—a taxi—as it zipped close behind her. Artie thrust his middle finger at the cab. The taxi's horn beeped twice.

"You son of a bitch!" Artie screamed. He ran into the street to look for a rock, but the cab was around the corner and out of sight before he could find one. He flexed his fists at his sides. "Nobody treats you like that when I'm around," he said to Jolene, his words coming out in a puff of fog. He cocked his head back and glared down the street where the cab had disappeared. There was only an occasional buttery window denting the darkness with its light. He kept his mouth shut because he thought it would make him look tough and sincere if he stood there with smoke coming out of his nose.

She moved her eyes back and forth, checking him over; then she bounced the donut bag in her hand as if trying to estimate its weight. She looked down at the sidewalk and traced a crack between two cement blocks with her brown pump. She didn't look at him when she spoke. "I got to get back, my baby's by himself, but . . . if you want to you can walk me home."

He breathed deeply and acted calm. He wanted to say something, something to set this hard and fast. But he couldn't think of the right words. So he smiled at her and took her arm and tried not to let himself shiver as she led him away. It looked good, he thought. He was hoping he wouldn't have to use any force.

# CHAPTER
# —3—

He checked out the back room of her apartment as if to be certain no one was waiting in ambush, peering into corners, noting the kid sleeping on the mattress. He returned to the kitchen and set a pint bottle of whiskey and a pack of Camels on the table. "Let's get to it," he said rubbing his hands together before cracking the cap on the liquor.

The words came out of her like something being unleashed; sentences rose like physical forces. Just talk talk talk talk talk. With only Dandy and the transistor radio to keep her company, she'd forgotten all about that joy. They discussed everything: ESP, UFOs, astrology. Reincarnation was a big topic. So was God. Neither one of them had ever seen Him.

"One thing for sure," Jolene said. "He wouldn't be caught dead in a dump like this."

"You think this is bad, wait till you see my place," Artie told her.

They discussed the color of each other's eyes and hair, listed all the rich and famous people who shared the colors with them, swapped more compliments, told more jokes. When making a point, they'd touch each other's arms briefly, as if unconsciously. Sometime after midnight they sang songs together. He knew mostly older ones she'd never heard of, and though he claimed to be familiar with the songs she knew, he had trouble with the lyrics. It didn't matter, since he was pretty good at making up his own words, which were funny, even if they were kind of dirty.

Once, he stood to show her a dance: the Funky Chicken. She laughed so hard she was afraid Dandy might wake up. Thank God he didn't.

It got to be three-thirty and the empty bottle stood on the table between them like a marker noting the end of something. All the sounds of the building—the noises of people moving and talking—had stopped. To Jolene, it felt like they were the only two people left alive in the world. She felt close to him. But when he said, "All right now, fun's fun, but let's get to the serious part," she wasn't sure what he meant. "Come on now, what's the story with this goddamned Henry guy?"

"You don't want to hear about that," she said, and she touched the bottle.

"Hey," he said, taking her hand and squeezing her fingers.

"No, I can't. I'd have to tell you all about my problem and you'd hate me."

"What problem?" He pushed back in his chair.

"It's not a problem I have now," she said, running an open palm over the surface of the kitchen table. "It's a problem I used to have. But it's all over with. Believe me, I don't have it anymore."

"What are you talking about?"

"I can't tell you, Artie. I don't even know you," she said. "If I tell you you'll hate me."

"Hate you? Why would I hate you? I know you got problems. That's why I'm here. I mean, guys come up to me on the streets all the time to tell me their problems. Everyone knows I'm the guy to fix things. I got politicians, for Chrissakes, calling me up, saying 'Artie, we're having trouble running the government. Can you help us out?' Some little problem you got won't mean nothing. Will it?"

She moved her head from side to side. "I don't know. . . . It's too soon to be talking about problems."

"Hey, it's never too soon to be honest. Now come on." He slid a cigarette across the table to her, and she covered it with her hand. "Give me a shot at it."

So she told him about her "amnesia." It wasn't like real amnesia, where she forgot who she was. It was more like she forgot she was *some*body and she'd find herself doing things—she didn't know why. She'd just like, sort of, wake up in the middle of a situation, and she never knew how she got there. Henry was her first husband—well, they weren't really married—and she met him in a gas station one day when she was making the rounds.

"Making the rounds?" he asked, jiggling nervously on the back legs of his chair.

She covered her eyes with her hands, her fingertips touching in the middle of her forehead, and looked at the rotted molding of the window beside the table. "I'd go into the ladies' room and keep the door open. I'd just stand there brushing my hair—I had long hair then—and kind of call out challenges to the guys. To join me." She ran her hands back over her head and drew them forward to cup her chin. When she glanced at Artie he seemed to be totaling things up with his eyes. She gave out a loud, dry sob and said, "I knew it, I knew I shouldn't have told you." She made her hands into fists and shook them. "I was just lonely, goddamn it. I was just looking for company."

He coughed and tapped his fingernail on the bottle, tapping it even while she looked at him, as if that flat clicking sound held the key to his understanding. "So what about Henry?" he asked. It sounded like he was jealous, which surprised and pleased her.

She stared at the table and let her eyes go unfocused. "Henry came in. He was the only one," she said. "I'd been to six gas stations and not one—not one guy would so much as shake my hand. It was always like that. All my life, no one would have anything to do with me. What am I, diseased?" She watched Artie slide the cigarette back across the table and light it for himself.

"What happened?" he asked, blowing smoke toward the ceiling.

"We, you know . . . did it . . . in the restroom. Then he took me to his apartment and let me stay there." She screwed the cap back onto the bottle, focusing her attention on it as she spoke. "I thought, This guy used to be in the Navy. He used to sail the seas all over the world. He'd seen all kinds of women, all colors and stuff. He was a real grown man and he picked me. That was the closest I'd ever been to love. . . ." She shook her head as if clearing it.

It wasn't enough. Artie had to know all the details. She kept asking why, what was the point? It was stupid. No good could come of it. He reassured her, told her it was for her sake, he was there to listen, he cared, he wouldn't use it against her. What else had she done? She had to admit it felt good talking about it and having him react the way he did. He shook his head and held her hand when she told him how Henry used to beat her and make her clean up after him when he was drunk and vomited. He stroked her hair when she told him about the phone calls from other women, about the nights Henry never came home. Of course she put up with it. You were supposed to put up with it, weren't you? Wasn't that what you did when you were dealing with love? She couldn't expect it to be perfect. Artie agreed with her eagerly and she went on.

She told him how things seemed to click for her when she found out she was pregnant. Henry told her to have an abortion, and when she refused he took back her key, then dragged her out and put her on the sidewalk; actually set her there with his hands like he was putting out a bag of trash. She decided, if he didn't need her, she didn't need him either. She went down to see the Welfare people and they gave her food stamps and found her a place to stay. She told herself that, starting right then and there, things were going to be different. She was almost eighteen. That made her an adult, and it was time for her to act like one.

First off, she was through with those situations she didn't know how she'd gotten into—like the gas station and other times—situations where she wasn't somebody else as much as she was nobody. Second off, she was going to have a baby who needed her. It wouldn't matter to him who the father was, or that he'd kicked them out. The baby was her accomplishment, and she was proud of it. She smiled and looked over her shoulder, as if she could see through the kitchen wall to watch the baby sleeping.

"Even at the hospital, when the doctors told me about his problem—the heart murmur and his little eyes, how they'll probably go blind—I didn't care. 'So what?' I said, everybody has problems. 'He's still dandy to me,' I told them, and that seemed to be the right name too, to let him know that he was okay. Dandy." She felt good, thinking about him, and she sat for a while, enjoying the feeling.

"Some changes you made," Artie said, standing and beginning to pace.

"That's for sure," Jolene said to the tabletop.

She didn't even understand now where it had come from. It was real complicated, but she tried to explain to Artie. It had something to do with knowing she'd gone through some roughness and didn't need to do it again; with feeling like she was worth something, maybe. Not because anybody else had decided she was—it was more like the opposite—but because she felt so herself. So what if she had to do things like wrestle at the Wrangler? She did what she had to. She was still worth something. At least she felt she was. God knew where that feeling came from, but it was there.

"Anyways, all that bad stuff is in the past," she said. Artie glanced at her with quick, shifting eyes, like a man plotting something. "I knew it," she said. "I shouldn't have told you."

"No, no, I'm glad you told me," he said, looking at the locks on the door. "I mean, so you're screwed up? So you did things no normal girl would ever do—gas stations and wrestling. So what? Just because you're a mess, that don't mean I'm gonna rub your face in it."

She couldn't help thinking it was all over. He was getting ready to leave. It was probably for the best. Not because of him, of any way he was. He seemed nice enough. He had tried hard to make her laugh, and he had listened without putting her down. But it was probably better not to get invovled with anyone. It would only turn out bad. "You can go if you want. Just don't hate me," she said.

"Hey." He stood before her. "I'm looking at you right here, right now. What's done is done." He sat and lifted her hand to his lap, then made cooing sounds. "Forget all that. Look at what you got now." He smiled and lifted his profile for her. When he spoke, it was in a soft, grating voice. "It's getting late now, darling. Time to get your kid out of the bed." His eyes bored right into hers, and she felt the sweat from his palms on her hands.

"Now be a gentleman," she said.

"What do you mean?"

"I'm not going to sleep with you, if that's what you're getting at."

"What're you talking about?" He let go of her hand and sat up in the chair. "What'd you go telling me all this stuff for? Getting me all excited."

"You asked me a question." When she sat up her head was higher than his. "I'm not like that. Even if I used to be, I'm not like that anymore. I never said I enjoyed it. I just did it."

He stood up and pushed the chair away roughly. "Oh man, I don't believe this."

"Artie, please, we've had a nice night. Treat me right, now."

"Treat me right," he said, spinning in a circle with his arms open. "Treat me right. Four in the morning, murderers on the street, and she's tossing me out," he told the refrigerator. "Who treat who right?"

"You can sleep on the floor out here, but you're not sleeping with me."

He banged his hand on the table and started to yell, his voice screechy, like an angry child's. She rose quickly, leaned into his face, and yelled back louder than he could. That scared him. He tried to hide his fear from her by moving around, avoiding her eyes. "I was just joking," he said. "I was just testing you. I mean, how could you respect me if I slept with you the first night. Ha ha."

She gave him one blanket, her only extra. He folded up a paper bag and used it for a pillow. It didn't seem to bother him; he told her he was grateful for the heat. He'd never had the heat turned on at his place because he couldn't afford the $100 deposit. And her bathroom was nice too. It wasn't out in the hall and it didn't smell. He said good night, went down on one knee, and kissed her hand. She had to laugh.

The next morning he left, swearing he'd be back in the afternoon. She didn't expect to see him again and spent the day sitting around with nothing to do but wait for Dandy to mess his diapers so that she could change them.

She was in the kitchen, watching Dandy as he knelt on the floor, moving his arms around in a patch of afternoon sunlight as if he were swimming through it. She thought that maybe Artie's leaving had nothing to do with her telling him about Henry or her problem, or making him stay in the kitchen. "The grief you cause me," she told her baby, nudging him with her toe. He raised his head and giggled.

A rapid knocking rattled the door. When she opened it, Artie was there with a glaze over his eyes and a small roll of bills in his hand.

"What's this?" she asked.

He winked and shook his head. "I have my means." He passed her a $5 bill. "This is for your boy, for whatever he needs. Now come on, gal, I'm taking you out on the town. I'm going to wine and dine you properly."

The shock of it flustered her, and all she could think to say was, "Where did the money come from?"

"Look, are you going to let me treat you right or not?"

She shook her head and looked around the room as if she expected guidance to come from the walls. "I guess, if we're going out, I should take a bath." She looked at Dandy.

"Well, go go *go,*" Artie said, looking at her baby. "I'll watch the kid." The smile stayed on his face but it seemed to change. He cleared his throat, then turned to her, his face brightening as an idea came to him. "You know, I should take a bath too, and it would only make sense, to save water—"

"Artie!"

He clapped his hands once. "Hey, you can't blame a guy for trying."

She sat in the bathtub, not even soaping up, just letting the hot water make her numb all over. It had been so long since she'd had a real date. Maybe she had *never* had a real date. She felt bad for herself. Was she some kind of freak? The hell with it. And the hell with where he got that money. She was going on a date now and she was going to enjoy herself. She couldn't understand, though, why he was so willing to spend money on her, when she wouldn't let him do anything. "Artie," she called.

"All right," he said. She watched as the bathroom door began to open.

"No, stay out. I didn't mean that."

"Jeez." He pulled the door shut again.

"Why do you want to spend money on me?" she called, sloshing some water over the edge of the tub onto the floor as she sat up.

She heard his feet shuffling and his fingers scratching at the wood of the door. "Goddamned gal. It's because you're—uh, you're—uh, the apple of my eye. You know? The butter on my toast. That sort of thing."

She slid down in the tub until her ears were underwater. "I'm not listening," she said. "I'm not paying any attention to that kind of talk." Not yet.

Everything happened too fast. Eggs and toast, meatball subs, Chinese food—and the eating was surrounded by a constant flow of drinking. She had never peed so much in her life. Though she'd never been a big drinker, it was free. And it was exciting to be going places with someone taking care of you, asking you what *you* wanted, telling you to try this, try that. Laughing and joking. It seemed he just wanted to make her happy. It was such a relief from having to look out for Dandy all the time. Then too, Artie didn't seem to really want anything from her but her company. She went along, feeling for the first time in her life that she could enjoy taking something without worrying about how she had to pay it back.

It went on for days. She wanted to see how far it would go, so she matched him glass for glass. Everything went by in a haze that made her actions seem distant, like she was watching herself in a movie. A funny movie. Even walking down the sidewalk was a good time, trying to balance on the lines or not hit any of the cracks. They drank in bars tucked away from the light in the mornings, in bars with TVs for the soap operas in the afternoons. At night he took her to Good Time Charley's, where the drinks were a little more expensive, but still cheap. Jolene was put off at first by the stripper there, and a few prostitutes hanging around the bar. But Artie told her nobody was there to see the show or do any business. He was right.

He even got her up to dance, something she hadn't done since junior high, when the school put on a yearly event in the gym. The walls and the ceilings would be decorated with crepe paper streamers, which always made her think of snakes that had been flattened by car tires and painted blue and pink. Even then she always danced with the other girls that none of the boys had asked. Once she danced with a boy, but it seemed he had done it on a dare, because he kept looking back at his friends, standing in a row along the wall, laughing. Her partner would dance Jolene around so her back faced the line of boys and then he'd grab her ass and try to lift her dress up. She finally let him do it, if it was that important to him. To all of them.

At first she was nervous about dancing with Artie. She didn't know how to hold herself, how to move. She didn't want to dance in a bar. There wasn't even a real dance floor, just a space in the back corner near the EXIT door. "People will laugh at us," she said.

"Hey gal, I'll never laugh at you," he told her. "So what, what they think. Nobody's going to laugh anyways. They know if they did they'd have to answer to me. I'm a respected man in here. Now loosen up." He was so intent on making sure she enjoyed herself that she gave in. They shuffled around in a slow embrace in the corner beneath the orange glow of the EXIT sign as the jukebox pounded out song after song of hard rock. Nobody paid them the slightest attention.

She was so caught up in having a good time that she even forgot she had a kid until each night was finished and it was time to go home. Dandy never seemed to mind being left alone. His bottle of milk or Coke, whatever Jolene had on hand, was always empty, and he had a mess to be changed, but he was never fussy.

On Saturday morning Artie told her, "You know, I done my best to be honorable to you. I spent all my hard-earned cash on you and I never complained. But I can't afford to keep two places. Denny's going to be out cruising tonight; he always is on Saturday. It'd be the perfect chance for me to split from him and hook up with you here. What do you say? I mean, you got to admit, we've been having a time for ourselves."

He was lying on the kitchen floor looking up at her. They'd both just awakened, and she was sitting at the table, balancing Dandy on her lap and wondering where Artie was going to take her for breakfast. The question was a surprise, and she wanted some time to think. She asked him, "What about Denny? Shouldn't you give him some notice?"

"Nah. But I'll be a nice guy and give him rent for the coming month. So I won't be able to help you out too much this first month—just this first month." He stretched out and folded his hands behind his head. "Besides, he did the same to me once. Booted a week before the rent came due. I had to pay it all myself."

"Why'd you move back with him, if he did that?" she said. Dandy made a noise as if he were about to whimper and she held him upside down, his head toward the floor, until he quieted.

"Are you serious?" Artie said. He rolled onto his stomach and barely managed a pushup. "He's my friend." He winked at Jolene and nodded for her to look at his muscle. His arms quivered and he dropped to the floor with a slam.

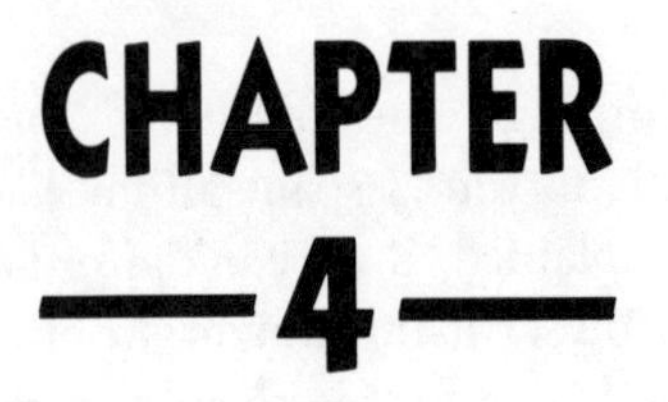

The street was a lineup of X-rated cinemas, storefronts selling fast food, dark barrooms with cracked wooden doorframes, and clothing stores displaying garish merchandise with crooked seams and loose threads advertised as "New York Fashions." Jolene knew the tags would say MADE IN INDIA.

"That's it," Artie said, and he pointed to the second-story window above a hot dog stand with white tiled walls, set in the lower corner of a tall gray building.

They left the street for a pitted alleyway. He stopped before a sunken door with a lock so loose it rattled as he turned the key. They climbed up the narrow, squeaking stairs. The pale green walls had so much plaster gouged from them it looked like there had been a mortar attack in there. One yellow bulb hung by a cord from the ceiling at the top of the stairs, swaying softly as if pushed by a breeze. The place spoke to Jolene of violence, mayhem. "Let's do this quick," she said to Artie.

His apartment door was thin plywood secured with a padlock. It had no handle. Artie undid the lock and pushed the door open. Inside, the darkness sat like a brooding creature, waiting for them.

"Oh my God," she said, standing in the middle of the room. A wave of disgust rose through her chest. She had an urge to bless herself, though she had never been that religious.

It was a nine-by-twelve cell. The one window was covered over by a nailed-up blanket, slightly skewed. Enough light slanted through the exposed triangle of glass at the top left corner to allow them to make their way around the room. When she looked at Artie she could only see the outline of his face. He was smiling. That made her nervous. She looked away.

On the floor beneath the window two mattresses lay end to end. Both were covered with thin blankets and newspapers, which had been opened out in overlapping layers. It looked like they'd been used for warmth. Taped on the walls above the mattresses, covering the space from the floor to the bottom of the window, were grainy magazine photographs. She knew what they were, even without being able to see them clearly. They became starkly visible as Artie yanked the blanket from the window to let in the glow from the streetlamp on the corner. The photographs showed women involved in degrading activities with men and dogs. Sometimes they were just exposing themselves to the camera. In other shots they stared straight ahead with drugged eyes and sperm spread over their faces, lips, and tongues.

The blue-white light from the streetlamp seemed to kindle smells in the room, which came to Jolene as two distinct odors: a heavy, pasty, bleachlike smell and the mingled stench of cooked meat and onions. What have you gotten yourself into now? she thought. Jolene, Jolene, now wake up, honey. What are you doing? Have you really slipped this low?

Artie saw her staring and turned to see what she was looking at. "Goddamn." He stepped onto one of the mattresses and stood between her and the photographs, making erasing motions with his hands. "Goddamn Denny. He always does this when I go away. He knows I don't like this shit. He's just trying to get me pissed." He looked over his shoulder at her, raising his eyebrows as if to see inside her mind.

She stepped backward, toward the door, and said, "I'll wait outside."

"Hey, come on now," he said, his voice rising into an angry whine. "What do you expect? A couple of swinging bachelors. Now come on now, Jolene. I ain't touched you in four days. I ain't forced nothing. Am I coming on to you now? Hell no. Now come on, didn't I take you out and show you the best time of your life?"

She halted and watched him. There was some truth there. Then she thought about what it would be like if she went home now, just her and Dandy, sitting in the kitchen, her talking to him and Dandy quiet like always. Nothing to do but listen to the transistor radio. She swore she knew the words to the ads better than she knew the songs. She thought about them just sitting there, watching out the window as the sun moved over the earth and nothing changed for her or her baby. She had never given a thought to how she spent her time until just now, and she felt panicky at the idea of going back to that. It's only been a few days with Artie, she thought. Why did it seem so much longer? How could he just work his way into her life in that short time? She saw herself and Artie as the two hands on a clock. She was the hour hand going slowly about her business, and he was the minute hand running around the same place as her, only faster. Every hour they'd line up together, even if only briefly. Something about that made her feel tender towards him.

"You got to take chances," Artie said, and she guessed he was right. You had to try something somewhere along the line. She wasn't waiting for any Princess Diana. No one was going to come riding into her life on a white horse, that was for sure.

Artie moved to the left front corner of the room and began to scavenge through a loose stack of clothing, the clothes heaped in a pile like raked-up leaves. She still felt jittery. Spasms in her neck made her head shake. A soft shuffling sounded behind her and she spun around.

A thin dark-skinned man stood in the doorway. His hands were folded across his chest, and one knee was bent forward, that foot balancing on its toes. Light defined the left side of his face. He looked foreign, and he wore a cream-colored nightshirt that might have been a dress. A sea-green beret was angled sideways on his head. "Moving?" he said, his voice soft and vibrant, as if the words were the first notes of a song. His features were delicate but seemed misformed, or aligned wrong. He spoke to Artie but checked out Jolene.

"Oh, it's you," Artie said. He smiled nervously.

"You were expecting the president?" The man shifted his weight to his other foot.

"You never can tell. He might call me." Artie laughed in his throat and stepped to the door. "Look—um, you got to leave me alone. I got to concentrate here."

"You got something for yourself?" the man said. He pointed his chin at Jolene. "Anything you care to share? I have no plans for the evening."

"Ha ha," Artie said. He swung the door to close it. The man stepped back into the hall, pouting.

"I'll miss you, Sweets," he called through the closed door, and then he laughed in a trilling, high-pitched burst. Artie slid the padlock through the inside hook to keep the door from being opened, but he didn't lock it.

"I think you owe me an explanation." Jolene stood in the middle of the room, all tensed up, her arms hugging herself as if she were afraid to brush up against anything. She felt there was a whole life here that could just seep into a person and take them over. Make it so they couldn't get out.

Artie looked up at the ceiling, circled the room with his eyes, then settled his gaze on her. "Some guy. Well, he used to be a guy; he had the operation and now he dresses up and gets work as a dancer. Denny gave him the nickname Lonely Boy, but his real name's George. You believe that? A Cuban named George? When he dances he calls himself Blaze Starr. But forget about him, okay? Now come on, Jolene, we got to get this done with so we can get home and celebrate *us*. We're starting our lives together, you know?"

"Just a minute, Artie." She felt on the verge of something important. He took her by the arms but she pulled away from him to think.

"Jolene, now." He shook his fists in the air. He grabbed a handful of her coat and pulled her down so he could kiss her face. "Remember? We agreed not to talk about the past."

"What past?" She pried his fingers open and took a step backward toward the door.

His back was to the window and his features were indistinct. She couldn't make out his eyes at all. When she looked up at the light coming in, a pain throbbed in her temple. She wasn't even sure anymore what this conversation was about. She felt an urge to get out of there as fast as she could. She felt outside forces grasping at them, not wanting to let go. She thought if they could just get out of there and be in daylight, things would be better. They might both be happy again.

"Look, the past starts in the last minute. It's already past. Your jelly donut this morning is the past. Everything's getting more and more past. Okay? All right? Now that that's clear, let's haul ass and get going before Denny comes back," he said.

"I thought you said he was gone."

"Jolene," he said. "This is his business office. Don't make me give you the details."

She nodded and looked around. She tried to reach for whatever had been working in her mind, but it was already gone. She saw a small shelved wooden table in the front corner, with a hot plate on top of it. An open can was on one burner, the top flared up and showing jagged edges. There was a movement on the side of the can, something small, a roach maybe, but it crawled around the back, out of her vision. Like a message from God it came into her skull then: I'm saving him.

"Look here," Artie said, as he pushed past her. He knelt before the table. She saw that the bottom shelf was covered with some sort of figurines. He picked one up but hesitated before handing it up to her. The skin on his forehead bunched and unfurled as he thought out his decision. Then he passed it back without looking at her. "This is the most important thing in my life." He faced the shelf. His voice was so reverent she wasn't even upset by the fact that she wasn't the most important thing. She opened her hand and saw a miniature terrior made of some sort of heavy gray metal. The features and fur were finely detailed. It almost looked alive.

"That one's pewter, but mostly I collect ceramic—some of them from Germany. And I also got some opalescent from Japan.

I got fifty-three of them, all different breeds. Well, some of them the same." He passed back another, then another, naming each dog and pointing out to her the ears, the eyes, all the details. He passed them back until her hands were full and she was afraid she would drop them. He kept talking and finally she had to interrupt to ask him to stop. He looked hurt, and she wanted to say something to show him she was interested, but what? She was ignorant about this whole area. All she could think of was, "You collect these, like a hobby?"

"Like a life," he said. "Since my uncle gave me a collie one time for my birthday. Well, it was really my father, but I call him my uncle sometimes, since he ain't always there. But he told me this dog was Lassie, but I knew it wasn't, on account of it was a male."

"But why?" she asked.

"Why? Because it had a dong."

"No, I mean why collect them?"

All his movements stilled as if he were slowing down his bodily processes. "Why? I don't know why. What kind of question is that? Do you go through your life asking yourself why?" A frightened look took over his face and he grabbed the dogs back from her quickly. He began wrapping them gently in the clothing he had picked from the pile. "Why, she says. People never bother with them 'cause they're little, but, you know, they're there." He held one up to make his point, then wrapped it in a sock. His hands moved with a delicacy she was shocked to see in him. "Why? They make me peaceful," he said, saying the words as if talking to the dogs. His voice was calmer. "They're something I like. I don't know. Something I know something about that not many other people do. Something that makes me different. Dogs too, you know? Man's best friend, all that. And they're so small, you know, it just . . . it gets you." His voice pulled tighter as he spoke. "Why'd you have to have a baby? Why'd Lonely Boy have an operation? Why do we go through all this shit? Why. I ain't no person to answer any goddamned whys." He clipped off the last word. The sounds of cars and sirens, of people's voices, came to them from outside as he rolled up the rest of the dogs in silence.

They piled everything inside a sheet and knotted the ends together so that it looked like a large hobo's bundle. Jolene agreed to lug it for Artie. "I don't want to throw my back out," he told her. "I got more important uses for those muscles." He gave her a knowing smile, but she only smiled back a little bit. When she didn't give him that big smile he had expected, it seemed to knock him out of line with himself.

Artie knew he needed to move in with her. You always took a free ride, wherever you could get it. But he wondered about it all the same. He was too happy. Maybe he was too involved. He knew he wasn't supposed to have any real feelings about her, but he couldn't deny the fun of the last four days; it had made him feel like a kid whose only worries were being in on time to eat. Even that hadn't been a problem with Jolene. They never set any times, just chowed down when they were hungry. Walking down the sidewalk beside her, he felt something had shifted in him, but he wasn't sure what. The cement blocks of the sidewalk reminded him of a game board. The squares might lead to something good at the end, but he had to make it past all the traps along the way.

It was a forty-five-minute walk down streets of apartment buildings that grew taller and narrower, whose bricks darkened from red to brown the farther they got away from the center. The stores and bars thinned until they passed only the occasional corner grocery, laundromat, or sandwich shop. When they were almost halfway there, Artie stopped in front of a liquor store and looked at the whiskey display in the front window. The bottles were arranged like a cityscape.

"Artie, maybe we should take it easy," Jolene said. She lowered the sheet to the ground and rubbed her shoulders. He watched her by her reflection beneath the word *Liquors*, glowing in a pink neon script.

"Are you trying to change me?" he said.

"No, honey, I'm must thinking we should start being careful

with our money. So we can save up for things."

"We need something to celebrate, gal. It's the start of a new life for us. How often does that happen? We got to celebrate, otherwise we'll jinx it." He rubbed his hands down his face and pushed on his eye sockets with his fingertips. "Do you have any money? I left mine at *our* place. *Our* place. You know, gal, that feels just like steak on my tongue." He poked his tongue out to show her.

He bought a fifth of St. Charles Fine California Brandy while she waited outside. He knew she wasn't crazy about hard stuff, but she couldn't say much about this now. It was a celebration-type drink. She wasn't too keen, though, when he cracked it open in the next block and ducked into the doorway of a boarded-up furniture store to slug some down.

"It's the cold, Jolene," he told her. She shifted the load from one shoulder to the other and shook her head at the sidewalk. "I got lean meat. I got to keep myself warm. You still got all your baby fat to pad you." He figured that would shut her up.

"I don't want to be the kind of people that other people stare at and make fun of later," she said. "Everybody can see us." She looked behind her, back down the way they'd come, then dropped her face and pulled her chin into her chest.

"It's nighttime. Who's going to see us?" Three young men in Western-style winter coats walked by. They all stared at Artie as they passed. He heard them snicker. "Look at this coat," he said loudly, hoping the men would hear. "Look how thin this is. I'm just being practical. You want to give me your coat, I won't drink. Okay? Now don't go being a nag before we even start living together."

He stopped three more times in the next fifteen minutes. Those were the shots he needed, too. To figure it all out. How to convince her on the rearrangements he had planned.

It took some talking, but finally he got her to put the kid out in the kitchen. "How can I be tender to you when I got this set of snake eyes watching my back?" Artie said. "And it's important for a boy to get his own room. I know. I'm a boy. You don't want him to grow up to be a faggot. You want him to grow up normal, like me. Right?" She finally stopped her whining and saw things his way. It wasn't bad for Artie at all. He had his own private room, which he shared with her, and a whole kitchen besides.

Thing is, he was a little spooked by the kid. Dandy wasn't the most normal-looking two-year-old Artie had ever seen. He had these thick glasses that looked like G.I.Q. Knickerbocker bottles, only not as brown, and his two eyes just crossed and floated around like each was on its own little trip somewhere. He'd point at something, and he'd keep moving the finger he was pointing with as if everything was getting away from him. Artie didn't know what the hell to make of it.

"He needs this operation," Jolene told him as they sat at the kitchen table. She balanced Dandy on her knee and took off his glasses. Dandy started shaking his head all around until Jolene held it steady and pointed it at Artie. "To straighten out his eyes for him. But the damn government won't pay. They say it's 'nonessential' because he can get by for now with the glasses. But the doctor told me, after a while he ain't going to be able to see nothing. All I can do is sit here and watch my baby go blind. And nobody's going to give me one penny until he can't see the hand in front of his face. All the money in the world won't do no good for Dandy then." She put the glasses back on the boy and he smiled.

"Maybe he'll be another Stevie Wonder. Can he sing?" Artie started in with the first line of "For Once in My Life," edging forward to try to get Dandy to sing too.

"Artie, don't you think we should get him to talk first?" Jolene said. She lifted Dandy so he stood on her leg. "And besides, who cares about a blind white boy? You got blind white people all over the streets. Everywhere you look you see someone tapping a cane. But the only time you see blind black people is when they're on TV singing. Stevie Wonder. Ray Charles. You ever see Stevie Wonder with a cane? No, they get record contracts. The white people get red and white canes." She became quiet, as if she were thinking.

Artie made his face look like he was concerned and thinking too. But the only thing going around in his mind was the liquor. Moving like a big furry wheel inside his brain.

"What do they expect from me? How am I supposed to come up with two thousand dollars?" she said.

Artie whistled. His breath rose and fell like the sound from a bomb. "You can only do what you can only do."

Jolene looked at him. "What?"

He shook his head. He looked at Dandy. The kid sat there, so quiet, looking confused, like he was searching for something. He almost never made a sound, never hardly cried. Maybe it was from being left alone all the time, Artie guessed. He didn't really know kids from Timbuktu. But the kid didn't seem like the way he was supposed to be. Like he didn't really turn out how anyone expected. Least of all himself. Artie stared at him and Dandy's eyes lined up correctly. He focused a gaze on Artie, a brief, penetrating look full of questions and accusations. Artie was spooked. He took another slug of brandy. I'll stare the little bastard down, he thought, but Dandy's eyes were already off on their journeys again.

"You going to help me with him?" Jolene asked. She lifted Dandy into his crib. It was a cardboard box that paper towels had been shipped in. The top was ripped off, and there were two blankets folded on the bottom for a mattress. The whole thing was wedged into the corner of the room, with the gas stove forming a third wall. Jolene put Dandy down and set a chair sideways in front of the box, so he couldn't tip it over. "Well?" she said to Artie. "He's *ours* now, you know."

"Ain't that something to think about," Artie said as he drank from the bottle. He ran his hand over the tabletop. "Well, of course I'm going to help." He felt warm and indistinct inside, and he pictured himself dropping Dandy out the window right into a trash barrel. Just like something in a cartoon. He laughed.

"What's so funny? Honey?" Jolene sat on his lap.

He groaned with her weight but kept on smiling. "Of course I'll help," he said. "I'm a man who knows his responsibilities."

He ran one hand down her leg and undid her bra through her T-shirt with his other hand. "Why, I'll take care of that boy just like I was his real father. Things are going to be so good. You're going to wish you met me when you were three years old. Just you wait. You'll see," he said, and he nuzzled his face to her shirt like a baby looking for the breast. "You aren't going to believe how your life's going to turn out now."

# CHAPTER —5—

By the middle of the second month they had $8 in cash and $10 worth of food stamps left. They were almost out of whiskey. Jolene seemed to be getting kind of twisted, Artie thought. Every time one of those sad songs came on the radio she'd blast it up and sing along, belting out the words as if she had an ache in her heart that wouldn't quit. He was worried. Then they were out of whiskey, and *he* started turning up them sad songs. Things were looking desperate.

"What do you want from me?" he said, breaking a silence that seemed to have stretched on for days. He twirled the empty fifth on the table and made believe that it would fill up again if he spun it long enough. "What do you expect?" he said.

"What are you talking about? Expect from what?" He ignored her. She was somewhere behind him, in the middle of the kitchen, probably playing with her goddamn kid like she'd done every single day Artie had been there until he was sick of it. She gave that kid some attention every three or four hours. Enough was goddamned enough.

There was a whimpering sound and Artie looked back at Dandy, who was trying to crawl. He was flat on his stomach, his head up against the broiler part of the stove, and his legs flapped and jerked. But he didn't go anywhere. "Can't you hush him up?" Artie said. "What's he crying about? He don't know problems from his ass."

"Artie! I told you before to watch your language around my boy. I don't want him talking like a sailor."

"Well, what'd you sleep with one for then?" he said. "Henry

goddamned Popeye." He put his eye to the top of the bottle and moved it around in his hands, as if it were a kaleidoscope.

"Are you talking about the past again?" she said. "For someone who says we're supposed to let it be, you talk about it all the time. What'd you do this for, what'd you do that for, on and on."

"That kid don't look like the past to me," Artie said. "Just get off my back."

Jolene grunted as she hefted Dandy from the floor. She sat him in the high chair across the table from Artie. Dandy was getting big, but she was able to squeeze him in. She wrapped his fingers around a spoon, opened the jar of peanut butter on the table, and moved the jar to his tray.

That's my peanut butter, Artie thought. I paid for that. It made him feel uneasy to think he couldn't go out and buy another one on his own. She'd have to give him the money. "You took my trade away from me," he said. "You took my pride with it."

"Thieving?" she said.

"It wasn't thieving. It was just B and Es. Them people had more stuff than I did. I was just passing it around in a fair way." She looked unconvinced, and he told her the only thing he could think of. "It was outdoor work, Jolene. Guys don't like to be cooped up, you know? Not like women. Guys, you know, need sun. Just like vegetables."

"You didn't seem to think it was so bad when I asked you to stop," she said. She pouted her lips out and shoved her shaking head at him. "Admit it."

Of course he wasn't about to admit it. When he had kicked in $20 toward the first month's rent, the money coming from a B & E he had pulled with Denny, she fussed at him for an entire night until he finally had to tell her so he could get some peace. He tried to explain then about how breaking into places was a trade, like anything else. She wouldn't have none of it. "You have to promise never to do that again," she said. "We have got to be a nice respectable family. We got to start living a regular life, like regular families are supposed to."

He hadn't minded at first. He liked having his time to himself.

Being able to enjoy a leisurely drink and a smoke in his own apartment. Messing around with Jolene during the daytime. They even went bowling twice, and he surprised himself by liking that too. Especially the game he won.

It got him to thinking about how tough things were getting on the street. Half the time he'd break into a place and there'd be nothing worth taking. Or the stuff was too heavy to haul out. Sully was getting cheap, too, about what he'd give you. He even refused a couple of good butcher knives Artie and Denny had lifted that last time.

"Who you think I'm selling to, friggin' housewives?" Sully told them. "These are for cutting tomatoes. Lookit the size of this." He lifted the knife off the counter in the pawn shop and pointed it at Artie's face, waving it like a sword. "Who are you supposed to be, Errol Flynn? Jumping around on rooftops fighting pirates? Bring me something practical, for Chrissakes. I'll give you a dollar for the bunch and that's it."

It was beginning to look to Artie like getting a gun was the way to go these days. Times changed. Of course, a gun—you're talking of staring some serious downtime in the face, and he didn't know if he was ready for that. A small guy like him. But hell, a guy his age couldn't crawl around on roofs and fire escapes forever. Even the purse bit was getting hazardous. With all the jogging and exercising he had to be really careful. Most of the girls could catch him, which was a problem no one had ever warned him about. It was a pretty screwed-up world, he thought, when a man couldn't make a living by his wits.

So of course he hadn't minded when Jolene pulled him out of the action. Not at first, he hadn't minded. He sat around trying to figure out some big scam to tide them over for a while. At least until Jolene decided to get a job. But just sitting in the apartment took his center away. He was out of touch with everyone and everything, all the bullshit and all the ideas, the energy that flowed when people sat around a bar talking about jobs to pull. He couldn't think of nothing.

Jolene stood up.

"Where you going?" he asked, looking at her sideways out of his slitted eyes.

"What are you, my fairy godmother? I have to tell you everything. You don't even answer my questions."

"Don't call me a fairy." He slammed his fist on the table. "Don't even say it fooling around."

"I'm going to check the mail," she said. He watched her slip out the door, leaving it open a crack, and listened to her footsteps fade as she descended.

Dandy was sitting up, holding the spoon, and he smiled in Artie's direction.

"Don't try to give me those eyes again, you son of a bitch," Artie said. He shaded his own eyes with one hand and reached across the table to pluck the spoon away from Dandy. Then he corraled the peanut butter with his arm and dragged it across the table. He sneered at Dandy and dug out a big spoonful. He wasn't even hungry, but goddamn it, it was his peanut butter. The one food he'd bought since they'd been together. You'd think Jolene could be more considerate, he told himself. She don't know nothing about attachments.

He thought he heard her footsteps, so he gagged down what was in his mouth and set the jar back on Dandy's tray. He put the spoon in Dandy's hand, but Dandy dropped it. Artie placed it in the kid's hand once more, and Dandy dropped it again. The footsteps were louder, closer, moving faster. "You trying to get me in trouble? Goddamn it, this ain't no game," Artie said, and he closed Dandy's fingers around the spoon, squeezing them as if they were made of clay and would stay together once they were molded. Dandy let go of the spoon and smiled with his tongue sticking out onto his chin. Artie picked up the spoon and Jolene walked in.

She looked at him and he looked back, openmouthed. Then he grinned and snapped his face around toward Dandy. He cooed out the words, "That's a good boy, eat all the peanut butter. Yup, eat all the peanut butter that Artie paid for. Yeah, good boy, yum yum. You want to eat all my fucking peanut butter?" When he saw Jolene wasn't watching, that she was reading a letter, he put the spoon off to the side of Dandy's tray, so the kid would have to fish for it. Slow him down.

As she read, Jolene's face brightened. It was like light shone off the paper and reflected from her skin. "Oh my God," she said. "Oh my God, Artie, you're not going to believe this. Do you believe in signs? I do, I do, and I swear this has got to be a please-dear-God sign."

She sat down to his right, at the table edge between Artie and Dandy, and read from the letter about the Miracle of Time Sharing. How, for less than what you would pay to own a new car, you could own—*own*—your own vacation home for *life!* "It says you can go to England, Greece, Switzerland—eighteen countries and thirty-seven states—any time you want to without paying any more than the 'small one-time purchase price.'" She read some more and turned to Artie, all excited; then her eyes sloped down with resignation. She reached over and held Dandy's hand to help him gouge a chunk out of the jar. "That'd sure be something nice to give my baby."

She looked at the letter again. "It says here, Artie, that you own the time you buy. One week, two weeks, or more. You own it forever, and you can do anything with it."

"Your whole life ain't a vacation," he told her. "What about the rest of your time?" He took the letter from her and spread it before him. There was an introductory paragraph and beneath that three columns, each listing three prizes. The top prize in each column was $750. They'd get one prize just for visiting and talking to a representative. He ran his tongue over his lips.

There was a number at the top of the letter to tell them which column their prize would come from. He looked at it for a while. He couldn't believe it. He ran one finger over that section of the letter to make sure it didn't rub off. It had to be the surest thing he'd seen in a long time. On this letter, instead of one winning number, there were two.

"They screwed up. Do you know what that means? Look here." He flapped the letter before her. "We're supposed to get one column, right? But they gave us two?" He leaned back and smiled. "Don't you see, Jolene?" He laughed and looked at her, and for some reason he was reminded of the way she looked that first night at the Wrangler, with her hair wet and stringy and the Jell-O smeared all over her face and neck and torso and legs. He could picture all that, and he felt a real concern for her skitter inside his chest. He did want to do something to make her happy. He did want to take care of her. As long as it didn't interfere with his options.

"We got that cash in our hands. I can feel it itching." Artie rubbed one palm with his fingertips. He wouldn't even let himself have any doubts. As he watched Jolene helping Dandy with the spoon, the idea of money for "them" receded, and Artie began to think about what he'd do with it. He had been the one to recognize the opportunity. It went right by her.

She slid the letter across the wooden surface of the table so that she could look at it again. "Dammit." She picked a large splinter out of her finger with her nails. "I'm sick of this table." She hit it with her fist. "Someday we're going to have a Formica tabletop." She studied the letter. "And someday we're going to have a real set of pans and dishes. And a TV. Everything real people have." She passed the letter back to Artie, shaking her head. "What makes you think we'll get the money?"

"That's the way it happens," he said, snapping the letter up and looking at it while he spoke. "People don't screw up unless they screw up all the way. It's a way of life. Take my word for it, I know about these things. Now don't just . . . just stop arguing with me."

She pulled at the skin of her throat and looked out the window at the building beside them. It was late afternoon, already turning dark, and the glass reflected their images and the bright yellow from the overhead fixture. "Seven hundred and fifty dollars," she said. "I bet that's enough to buy one of those places."

"Yeah, well, there might be better uses for that money." Artie coughed. He imagined the feel of the bills in his hands—he'd get nothing bigger than a ten. Well, maybe a few twenties to sandwich the stack. But mostly tens, so he'd have a nice fat roll to show. He thought of the soft, cracking sound the bills would make as he flipped through them. He didn't know what he'd do with the cash. Sure, he'd share some with her, so she could buy what she wanted. Groceries and stuff. But fair is fair, and anyone could see that most of it should be his. He did the thinking.

"Maybe the doctors could fix up one of his eyes," she said.

"Let's not waste it," Artie told her. "You like music—buy yourself a real good radio with speakers."

She turned to her son. "Oh, damn you, Dandy. You're making a mess."

Artie looked over at the kid. He was smooshing one fat little hand into the peanut butter on the spoon, then rubbing that hand across his face until he found his mouth. There were brown streaks all over his face and clothes. "Hell, that kid ain't making no mess, he's just being resourceful," Artie said, laughing. "What're you getting upset for? It won't take you a minute to clean him." He felt generous, now that he knew he was going to be a man of means. Like it was all right that the kid wasn't his, and that the kid was screwed up, and that Jolene really liked the kid. Everything looked acceptable when you had money, he thought. But when he looked at Jolene he realized this might be it for them. He might have to leave her. Find another woman who had money to match his own. The idea of leaving her unsettled him, and he felt sad about it. As if he already missed her.

"Do you want to clean him?" she asked.

"He's your kid," Artie said. He looked at Dandy. Jolene had moved the peanut butter away from him and he was reaching out like a blind man, trying to find it. "You should give him *more* food, for being resourceful."

"What do you know about resourceful?" she snapped. "Nothing. And when was the last time you helped me around here?"

His blood thickened up. Here he was thinking good thoughts about her, and all she wanted to do was put him down. "Shows what you know," he informed her. "In my circles I'm considered quite a genius at resourceful."

"In your circles," she said. "You haven't left this apartment in four weeks except to go to the packy for another bottle." She wiped Dandy's face with one of the napkins from a stack she had stolen from Burger King. She spit on the napkin, then rubbed his skin with it. "Only thing I've seen you circle is that liquor and my AFDC check."

He sat there, staring at the back of her head as she cleaned off her kid. He felt like punching her while her face was turned, but he didn't want to hit her. He hadn't hit her yet and he didn't want to get started. That always seemed to change things. He looked at the letter—it was addressed to Mrs. Jolene Handy—and he closed his eyes and counted silently to four. He set a troubled look on his face and stood up, lifting his jacket from the back of his chair.

"Where you going to?" she asked.

"Things I do for you and you don't even appreciate them. But that's all right. I don't care. I'm not going to mention the time I stole a whole stack of toilet paper from the Sunoco station and had to walk down the street with my arms full. Had to look like a fool. But I did it for you—and don't try denying that you use more than I do; you wipe when you pee and I don't. Or how about the time I took the ketchup packets—twenty-three, remember? And the girl behind the counter in her little McDonald's hat yelling at me the whole time I was running out the door? Or what about the steaks I shoved down my pants? But no, these things don't mean nothing to you." He sighed and shook his head. He stared at the floor as if waiting for it to open up on him. "I love you so much, Jolene, I can't stand to see you sad. So if I'm the cause of your sorrow, I'll be on my way. I'll go stand in some cold doorway or something, maybe I'll freeze to death—but hey, I'm not putting that on you. It's my decision. But if it'll make you happier . . ." He shook his head and slipped his jacket on, then zipped it up, trembling with an exaggerated shiver, and looked mournfully at the ceiling.

"Artie, don't be ridiculous." Jolene put her fingertips to the table, making a shelter form out of her hand. They stood in the quiet for some time, not looking at each other. She was still looking at her hand when she spoke. "I'm sorry I was nasty to you. It's just, I'm just . . . I don't know. I guess I'm worried that once you get some money in your hand you'll be gone and it'll just be me and Dandy again."

He lifted her hand from the table and kissed it, then held it to his cheek, like he had seen in a movie one time. He cleared his throat so he could talk softer. But he swallowed his mucus. He thought if he spit it out now it might break the mood. "I ain't going to leave you. Hell, I'd do anything for you, gal. I ain't never loved a woman like I love you, Jolene."

"Quit it now," she said, looking down at him. Her eyes told him she was weakening.

"Hey no, gal, I mean it. I been with women in my time, and I felt like what I thought was love. And you ain't the most beautiful woman I ever known, and even though you got a screwed-up past so that most men wouldn't touch you with a ten-foot pole—I don't care about none of that. Because since I met you I realize I ain't never loved nobody. Before. And I'll help you. I'll help dry the dishes sometimes, carry the laundry—when my back ain't hurting. Make the sandwiches and heat up the soup once in a while. Just give me some time to think about it. I've never said that to anyone before. But gal, I love you so much I don't care about my own pride. And if you were to die, why, I would kill myself, because I could not go on. Like that song says." In a low, growly voice he sang to her about how his love would still exist even when the mountains had all crumbled to the sea, and the seas had all dried up, and life, as they knew it, had ceased to exist, except for the dolphins.

"Artie, if I died you wouldn't really kill yourself, would you?" She looked at him; her forehead was wrinkled and her eyebrows pulled together so that they angled down and touched. But she was happy, too.

"Hey gal, what would be left for me? Life without you is like no life at all. It's like the soup without the sandwich."

"Nobody ever said things like that to me," she told him.

"I bet," he said. "And I mean it." He still held her hand to his face. She rubbed her other hand over his cheek.

"Honey," she said, "if I died I'd want you to stay and take care of Dandy."

"I would rather die," he said. "But baby, I would do whatever you asked me to. I mean it. Everything I said. Even what I don't remember." He did mean it, too. In his own way. Of course, he wouldn't kill himself. But he would mourn for her and want to keep things to remember her by, like the radio and the toaster. But nix on the kid.

"You know, the only thing we ever fight about, really fight about, is money," she said. "Let's not ever fight again."

He smiled and pulled her closer. He stood on his toes and tongued her and began feeling her up. She leaned away from him and nodded across toward Dandy. In an amused, put-off voice she said, "Artie!"

They put Dandy away for the night and then Artie and Jolene walked through the open doorway into the other room. There was the mattress on the floor and, beside that, an overturned milk case with an alarm clock and two paper coffee cups on it. On the far side of the room, diagonally across from the corner the mattress was in, was the closet, a long wide one with sliding double doors. One door was open and clothes had fallen out in a loose heap, as if they'd been tossed about in a burglary. Only two dresses hung from the bunched metal hangers hooked on the clothes bar.

A bulb glared from its sunken socket in the middle of the ceiling; the light made stretched half circles of shadow in the corners of the room. Jolene looked at everything, squinting her eyes, like she thought there was some inner life there, waiting to reveal itself to her. She shook her head and snapped off the bulb.

They dropped their clothes in separate piles at the foot of the mattress and scrambled under the blankets.

Artie kissed her neck slowly, touching his lips from the side to the front to the other side and back to the front again. He moved his hands gently over her breasts and kissed his way up to her ears. He watched the breath rise from her mouth like a small cloud of mist. "It'll be all right," he said. "I'll take care of you."

"Oh God, what's going to happen to us?" Jolene's eyes were closed. She reached over for him.

He was ready and he didn't want to get into another scene, so he let that go. He was too caught up in being there with her to give it much thought. He moved his hands all over her as they rolled together. "I ain't never had a woman that loved like you," he told her. It was true. It was like she put her whole self into it. She loved like she could never stop. She loved so hard and true . . . like she wanted to make one part of her life perfect. Then maybe the rest would be pulled along and fall into place too.

They went on until Artie was too tired to go any longer. Finishing with a long, slow shiver, he lay atop her for a while. Slowly he let himself fall away, rolling onto his back. He tried to think of the first time he'd seen her. But he kept passing in and out of sleep so that the events took on a drug-warped sense, memory mixing with dream. He wasn't sure what was real and what his mind was working on. The last thing he remembered clearly was Jolene rolling away to lie on her side, her face pressed to the pillow. He could hear those soft, short sounds like she was sobbing. But God, he was too tired. . . .

He was at the Wrangler, with the crowd and the noise all around him, and the wrestling about to start. "Oh boy," he said to the person beside him. It was a woman, but when she turned she had no eyes, nose, mouth, or ears: just a rounded, face-shaped form. That disturbed him and he stood up to leave.

But as he turned to go he found his feet were glued to the floor. He couldn't tear them loose. He looked up and saw the Saints moving for him, laughing, and he yelled "No no no no no." He kept trying to rip his feet loose but they wouldn't budge. The Saints drew closer, tipping over tables and chairs, some of them swinging chains and pool cues. The Sin City Strapper led the way. Her top was down but instead of breasts a pair of snarling, saw-toothed creatures pushed from her chest, snapping for Artie's flesh. He looked up and saw she had no features on her face either, but she kept calling him. The noise echoed inside his skull. "Come to mama, come to mama," she called. She grabbed his head and pulled him closer to the flashing, saliva-glinting teeth.

His thrashing woke Jolene, but not all the way. She flopped her head over to face him, fluttering her eyes, screwing up her face; through the thick unconsciousness of her own sleep she asked, "Who are you?" Then she was gone.

Artie looked at the ceiling, remembering little from his dream but the feeling of terror. He examined the nicks and craters and cracks, the peeling flakes of paint, all of it just visible in the dusky predawn air. A cold swirl sniffed around the edges of the mattress, slinking under the blanket to chill his skin each time he shifted. He tried not to move. He crossed his hands at the wrists and held the blankets tight to his chin. He lay there watching, afraid to go back to sleep, as the room slowly came to light with the morning.

# CHAPTER
# —6—

Their appointment was for a Tuesday, a cold brisk day with a packed gray sky threatening snow. On the drive down he almost thought they were on another planet. It was like nothing he had ever seen. He could tell Jolene felt the same, because she had stopped fiddling the radio from station to station and was just sitting there with her face pressed to the side window, not saying a word. The more they drove the more uncertain Artie felt. All that richness. It was like he was losing his bearings. He felt out of touch with his life, with everything familiar to him. He was afraid, too, that Smitty's car wouldn't last out the ride.

"You see this stuff on TV," Jolene said as they traveled past miles of trees and bushes, thick and green. A clearing opened suddenly and they drove past a Queen Anne house with a columned porch running all the way around it. "If you have a TV," she added. The house had a long rolling yard landscaped with trees and shrubbery. A fountain was centered on the lawn like a giant crystallized flower.

"Oh, Artie," she said.

"Look at that one!" He pointed as they drove past an immense mock-Gothic with pointed-arch windows, elaborate porch supports, and castellations above the porch. The three center sections were flanked by battlements. "There's got to be fifteen windows there," Artie said.

"It looks like a castle."

"You could fit all the overnighters from Sal's in there and still have room left over."

"Real people live in there," Jolene said. She spoke softly.

"Families. People who know each other." She turned and watched as the house disappeared behind them. Then she reached her hand out toward Dandy, who lay on the back seat. She wiggled her fingers in front of his face and he smiled.

"It ain't like the city," Artie said. "It's like the Twilight Zone." She gave a small laugh but he hadn't meant it to be funny. He felt like they were trapped somewhere, some place not quite real. Or in a different dimension. Or maybe they were just dreaming and they couldn't wake up and see what it was really like. He glanced at Jolene. She had a lost look on her face, like she was in some place far beyond him. He began to worry, and his fear sucked away his confidence.

"Oh God, this has got to work," she said. "Something's got to work. We need something." She watched as they rolled past a few more houses. "I feel so small." She brought a hand to her mouth and gnawed on her nails.

"What a thing to say," he told her. He slapped the dash. "Don't go bringing no bad luck down on me."

The building was a compact, weathered-looking Cape, with blue shutters and a simple white door. There was an empty twenty-car parking lot fronting it. The tar was a rich charcoal color, the lines marking the spaces a bright mustard.

Artie wheeled Smitty's station wagon into a space beneath the window to the right of the door. Nailed to the building was a white sign with red lettering: 20th Century Time Sharing, Inc. Beneath that a glass-encased message board displayed fifty or so photographs of what looked to be families and couples. The black heading of the board said *Happy Lifemates.*

"Artie, this isn't going to work. We're out of place here. Let's just go, honey, while we can. We don't belong here. This is a whole different world. We got no place here."

"Goddamn it, gal, don't step on my luck." He tried to pump himself up, but he could feel that something had drained away. He said, "*They* screwed up. We're in control here. Be positive. What's the worst that can happen?" His voice sounded so weak he felt ashamed.

She looked out the window, then back at him, then slumped her face into her hands and shook her head. He lifted the letter from her lap.

"Look," he said. "The absolute worst, we get the—um, ratchet wrench set and the thirty-five millimeter camera. Sully's got to give me at least a ten spot for a good wrench set and seventy-five dollars for a new camera." No sense bringing up now the agreement he'd had to make with Smitty, to split with him for letting him take Smitty's car. "Cut out twelve bucks for gas."

"What good is seventy-three dollars?" she asked.

"Shut up, Jolene, I'm thinking."

"You don't have to yell at me. You've been doing that an awful lot lately and I'm getting tired of it."

He rubbed his chin with his hand. "You got a better scam?"

She put her hands on the dash, settling them slowly as if she were about to play the piano, and tucked her chin into her chest. "I don't want a scam. I want something we can plan on. I want to look at what we got and be able to look ahead to what we're going to have. This can't go on."

Artie could see the shape of someone behind the window curtain. Whoever it was, was staring out at them. He told Jolene, "You know, J. P. Getty didn't start off with no million dollars, I bet. He probably started off with seventy-three dollars too. He probably started off just like us."

"Artie." She made a smacking noise with her lips.

"What?" he said, and he smacked his lips back at her.

"You always miss the obvious things."

"What obvious things?"

"He lived in Texas," she said.

He waited for more, but when she didn't say anything else he asked, "So?"

"So it's hot down there. It don't cost so much. You don't have to spend money on heat and buy all these clothes and things."

"That's right," he said. "It's the little things. Like your makeup."

"Like your whiskey."

"That's enough, Jolene," he said, and he hopped out of the car and slammed the door behind him.

They were hustled right through the small reception area, with its photograph-covered walls and the middle-aged woman sitting at the metal desk reading a paperback. The guy who took control of them led them straight into the open center room. There was a doorway to a back room, but it was dark and they couldn't see in. "I suppose I can talk to you," he said. "Fortunately for you I have some free time." He motioned for them to sit at one of the three white cafe tables in the room. The tables were spaced ten feet apart on the blue carpeting, which ran from one bare cream-colored wall to the other. Blue plastic chairs surrounded the tables. "My name's Mr. William T. Gristel," the man said. He picked over Artie with his eyes. "This should be amusing."

The guy was real slick, Artie thought. He had short, neat hair, all his teeth, and no scars on his face. A thick, spicy odor oozed off of him. He had Artie beat by a good six inches in height. Artie was unnerved by it all, but he looked up at the guy and nodded his head, to show Gristel that he, Artie, knew something. "That's why we came," Artie said. "To be amusing."

Jolene bent over and hiked up Dandy's corduroys for him. She pulled down on his flannel shirt with one hand to smooth it out. With her other hand she kept him steady on his feet, but he tottered as if he could fall at any second. She was wearing a pair of stretch slacks the color of swimming-pool water, and when she bent over the slacks pulled tight around her ass. Artie was enjoying the view; then he got worried that Gristel might be too. But when he glanced over, Mr. William T. Gristel looked back at Artie with a face of impassive confidence.

Jolene straightened up with an apologizing smile on her face. She looked at Gristel as if asking him to forgive her for even being there. She held Dandy's hands to keep him from falling as he stumbled around the floor. Artie felt like screaming at her. This was no time to be teaching the kid how to walk. This was no time to be apologizing. She moved to Artie and picked something off the shoulder of his jacket, then started brushing at some small stain on the front of Artie's work shirt. He'd just about had it with her. She told Mr. Gristel, "He just spilled some coffee on the way down, that's why he's messy." Artie closed his eyes and clenched his fists for control.

The guy took it in without a word, but Artie had to work to keep the smile on his face. Goddamn Jolene, he thought, with her picking and all. And damn this guy, with his fancy suit and matching hanky, his cuff links and gold tie clip, his way, when he did say something, of dishing out words like he was doing them a favor. . . .

He made Artie and Jolene sit at one of the tables and fill out forms—addresses, jobs, income, etc. He watched over Artie's shoulder the whole time, smiling and correcting Artie's spelling. He smirked when Artie had to ask Jolene for their address. He laughed out loud when Artie wrote he was between jobs and looking over his options. "Rambler station wagon?" Mr. Gristel said as Artie wrote in Smitty's car for his own. "Still running after twenty years, huh?"

"It runs like a charm. Built to last," Artie said. He didn't know what the guy was getting at. "It's a valuable antique."

"Oh, unquestionably," Mr. Gristel said, and he walked in a circle, snorting to himself and jingling the change in his pockets.

He took their completed forms, excused himself for a minute, and stepped into the back room. Artie heard voices from there, talking low, then a lot of loud laughter. Jolene went "pssst" to get his attention, but he wouldn't look at her. He just stared down at his boots.

"Well, we'll get your prizes so you can leave," Mr. Gristel said as he crossed the room to stand before them. His hands were in his pants pockets and he rocked on his heels.

Jolene bounced Dandy on her lap and glanced at Artie with relief. But he gave her a sharp look to shut her up. He didn't want to hear anything she had to say.

"No sirree," Artie said, and he gave Jolene a slow wink. "We're here to buy us a vacation home. I'm a man of some means. I got a little something tucked away from when I worked for the government, and I told the missus I'd buy her something real nice for our anniversary."

"What are you doing?" Jolene said. Her face twisted with disgust and confusion. Artie couldn'ye popped her one.

"What am I doing? What are you doing?" he whispered to her savagely. Then he smiled at Gristel and delicately crossed his legs and folded his hands over one knee.

"Yes, some means," Gristel said. "I'm certain." He turned to Jolene. "When is your anniversary? Which one are you celebrating?"

"Artie, let's just—"

"Shut up!" he warned her. He gave Gristel his best smile and said, "It's soon."

"Did you say June?"

"Yeah, that's right. June."

Mr. Gristel looked amused. He faced Jolene, stared at her. She became uncomfortable and finally told him. "It's our first." Gristel nodded. He looked at Dandy, then he watched Artie fidget in his chair.

Mr. Gristel peered down at Dandy. "That's nice . . . that's a real . . ." He smiled at Artie. "Is that your boy there?"

Artie had just about had it with this guy. He wanted to let him know he meant business. He wanted this Mr. Gristel to treat him like he would all the others. All his life he'd had to put up with this kind of shit, everyone talking down at him all the time. He'd had enough of it. He pushed up from his chair and said, "Look, are you going to show us these joints, or do we have to spend our money elsewhere?"

"Heaven forbid! I wouldn't want you to spend your fortune elsewhere." He voiced the words in a large manner, as if he were on stage. "Sit. Sit. Let me bring out the books."

Jolene put a steady gaze on Artie as Gristel left. She didn't say a word and he tipped back in his chair, arms folded before him, and glared across the room at her. She broke the gaze and brushed the hair off Dandy's forehead.

Mr. Gristel brought out two three-ring photo albums. He explained to them all about time sharing. How you bought a week of a house, the same week every year, and you owned that house for that week forever. Well, it was really a condominium, but it was every bit as private as a house and it was yours forever. And you only paid a small maintenance fee every year for the rest of your life—he couldn't recall exactly what it was, but it was negligible. All you really had to pay was the one-time price for the unit. Just once and that was it. Except, of course, for your share of taxes, but the rates were just so low here it wasn't worth considering. But anyway, you owned that house forever. Forever. And . . . And . . . *you* had the right, and here was the beauty of it, to trade any time you wanted with someone who had a different week, or swap with someone who had a week in a faraway country you always wanted to visit. Or Bermuda or Disneyland—and wouldn't the boy like that? Experiences like that are priceless for a child. The options are endless, he said, and he smiled expressly at Artie. "Time sharing," he told them. "It's the only way."

Artie supposed it would be good if you were only alive one week a year, but what would you do with the rest of your weeks? He had questions about sharing it, too. Of course Jolene would keep the place neat, but what if there were other people like them who owned it and wouldn't? He asked about that and Mr. Gristel shook his head and smiled at Jolene. "Of course people will take care of it. People always take care of what they own," he said.

Artie knew that wasn't true. But he didn't say anything.

The guy went on, and Artie didn't pay too much attention. He leaned back in his chair and felt removed from it all. When Gristel looked at him, Artie would nod or say "Yeah," but mostly he was talking to Jolene. Artie knew for her it was like being at the movies. She couldn't tell it wasn't real. All those pictures they had of happy couples and families having barbecues and stuff. Everyone who had bought in. When Gristel got to those pictures of faraway places, mountains and lakes and things, Artie thought Jolene was going to cry. He pinched her arm but she brushed his hand off and paid him no mind.

Mr. Gristel gave her a couple of photographs to keep, and she stuck them right down into her pocket, away from Artie. No matter. He figured he could rustle them up when they were back at the apartment. He found plenty of things by looking around when she was in the bath.

Gristel's car was in the back lot. It was a Cadillac, as big as an apartment and with seats so soft you swore you'd sink in until you were lost. There was music floating all around and Artie felt like he was in heaven. They drove down a bumpy dirt road, full of curves and potholes, but the ride was smooth. They stopped at a six-unit place, the building winding snakelike through a grove of pine trees. When they stopped the car in the muddy front yard they had to wait awhile for Jolene to leave the back seat. She kept feeling the cushions and closing her eyes.

The building was new and the sharp scent of cut wood still hung in the air. The plank walls were stained natural, and there were light blue shutters on the windows, and blue doors. It looked like what Artie thought of as the Wild West.

Well, the outsides were fine, Artie thought, as they followed Gristel through the door. The insides, though, were something else. The last time he had seen anything like it was on some TV show he caught in a bar somewhere. Dishwasher, washing machine, dryer, microwave, fireplace, built-in bar, stereo, color TV with cable, a kitchen with two glass walls, a porch running the length of the back of the living room, spiral stairs leading up to three bedrooms, carpeting everywhere so thick it didn't even feel like there was a floor beneath it. And the furniture. It was so nice Artie was almost afraid to sit on it.

"Gorgeous, isn't it?" Mr. Gristel said as they stood in the living room. "Real class. Go ahead, you're allowed to sit."

"Almost as good as our stuff," Artie said, touching the top of the TV. He wanted to switch it on, just to see something in color. Gristel gave him a smile and an arched eyebrow. Artie stepped back and said, "The stuff in our guest room." Gristel shook his head and crossed the room to Jolene.

Jolene sat slowly on the couch. She moved carefully, as if she didn't want to leave an imprint. She sat on the edge of the couch and ran her hands over the plush velveteen cushions. Mr. Gristel clicked on the stereo. It was an all-music soft-sounds station, and the music filled the room. He pointed at the four speakers, set into the walls at the corners near the ceiling. "There are speakers in every room."

"In every room?" Jolene said. She looked at him as if he had just announced a cure for cancer.

"Every single room."

Artie hopped onto the rocking chair on his side of the room. He cranked back, to show her it was all right, they could use that furniture. After all, they were company. She didn't give him any attention. He was getting riled. She hadn't hardly spoken to him since they'd arrived. All she'd done was mess around with Dandy and talk to Gristel. What was she thinking? No way was she going to go home with that guy, Artie told himself.

"We live in a two-room fourth-floor walkup," Jolene said.

"Hey now! Nobody wants to hear that," Artie said. He looked at Gristel. "Nothing wrong with that. Good for you. Women don't like to exercise, you know?"

"My wife jogs five miles a day," Gristel told him.

"What do you know? It's like Sherwood Forest out here. You can't do that where we live. They got dogs, crapping all over the place. You can't even walk, for Chrissakes. It's everywhere. And in the summer, the stink, you'd swear it was seeping out of the sidewalks. A day don't go by when you don't get some smooshed all over your shoes—"

"Artie, please, for God's sake. I've got some pride," Jolene said.

That made Artie mad. He was just entertaining the guy, trying to get Gristel's mind off the mistake she'd made in telling him the truth. He was ready to say something to Jolene, but he figured he'd better keep his mouth shut for now. He couldn't look at her, though, without his anger showing, so he turned to Dandy, who was off in the far corner of the room, beside the rubber tree. Dandy had his arms pressed against the wall for balance. He was stooping and grunting. Then he climbed his hands up until he was almost standing and stomped his leg to work something out the pantleg of his loose trousers. "Speak of the devil," Artie said, and he gave a big laugh.

"That takes the cake," Gristel said. He had a look on his face. Not just upset, but like he should've expected something like this to happen.

"This ain't my kid," Artie was quick to tell him. "My kid would have more class."

Jolene rushed over to Dandy. She took a Kleenex from her pocket and picked something off the rug. She turned on Artie, her movements as sharp as a straight-edged razor. "My kid isn't good enough for you? Is that what you're saying? Answer me, goddamn you."

"I didn't say that."

"You're awful quick with your mouth against me and my own until *you* need something."

"Now whoa, for Chrissakes. That ain't true. Tell him it ain't true. I don't want this guy thinking lies about me." He leaned forward, then pushed himself back to hold in his rage. He told Gristel, "Don't think I'm saying it's Jolene's fault, cause it ain't. It's the father. Biology, you know? You know biology?"

Gristel looked at the stain on the rug, then turned back to Artie. His lips puckered out in a tight smile. He nodded slowly. "I think so."

"Good," Artie told him. "It's important to be on the same level. The kid takes after his father is what I'm saying." He watched Jolene catch Dandy up under her arms and carry him from the room.

"Oh?" Gristel said. "The father messes his pants?"

That shook him. Artie tried to look hard at Mr. Gristel's eyes, but the guy was good at that game and Artie had to turn away. "That's right," he said. He wondered if Gristel was a simple son of a bitch or what. What was he getting at? On the wall across from him, beneath a line of track lights, was a color print of a pair of ballet shoes, old and dirty, one crossed over the other. Artie pretended to be appreciating it.

The water burst on in the bathroom down the hallway. Jolene

screamed, "What do you know about my boy's father? That man was man enough to almost marry me. He kept himself working, too, which was more than I can say for you. He was a good man, except for the liquor and the women."

Artie listened to the splashing sounds. He knew she was wringing out Dandy's underpants. They'd been out of diapers when they woke, and Dandy had already done a mess, so she decided to take a chance on him lasting out the visit. Artie knew she had forgotten to bring an extra pair of underwear for her kid, but it wasn't his job to remind her. It was her kid. He didn't want her to start depending on him to do things for her. Once that got started there'd be no stopping her from taking advantage of his good nature.

Gristel was staring at him, rocking on his heels and looking down his nose. His lips were closed seriously and the first signs of jowls showed at his jawline. A smile quivered across Artie's face. "That kid," Artie said, shaking his head.

"That kid?" Gristel asked. He raised his eyebrows. He wouldn't stop staring, and Artie shifted in his chair and cleared his throat.

"Yeah, that kid," Artie said. "Usually he does it right after we eat. He thinks we can't figure it out, but I know what he's up to." He nodded and Gristel nodded with him.

"You do?" Gristel said.

"That's right," Artie told him. "He can't fool me."

"He thinks he can fool you, but you're smart enough to figure him out?" Gristel said, waving a finger above his head.

"Sure. He knows Jolene's going to be with me at night and he's just trying to snatch back her attention for himself."

Mr. Gristel laughed out loud, shook his head, and turned on his heel. Artie sunk his chin in one hand and tried to figure that one out.

He listened to Dandy's whimpering, then Jolene came to the doorway by the couch. She looked across the room at Artie. Her face was red and mad, but her eyes were still wide as they took in the place one more time. The breath seemed to suck out of her, and that gave him the impression she was shrinking. Her shoulders hunched forward and her head sagged lower. She turned to Gristel and said, "I am really so sorry, sir, for everything."

"It's okay. We pay people to clean these units. It's about time they started to earn their salaries."

"No, really, sir, if there was anything I could do to make it up to you. I am so humiliated. You don't know."

"Forget it," he said, jingling his change.

"Truly, sir, I did not mean to come in here and be such a problem. I didn't even want to come in once we got here. I knew it was a mistake. I mean, anybody can tell."

"Oh, everything's all right. Don't worry about it. Now, let's get you going." He touched her elbow and turned her toward the door.

Artie wanted to see the racquetball courts and the indoor pool, the sauna and the Jacuzzi. All those things he'd never seen. But there was a slippery feeling about everything; it was all pulling away from him, and he didn't know exactly how to get back in control.

He couldn't believe it. The wrench set fit in the palm of his hand and the camera, which was no bigger, had a lens the size of a quarter. They were both made in Taiwan. He raised a stink. "What do you think, I'm a midget? What kind of respect is this?"

"Oh, come on now. You have no complaint," Mr. Gristel said wearily.

"Artie, please. Enough is enough for one day," Jolene said. She tugged on his arm.

"Look, even your friend here is sick of listening to you," Gristel told him.

Artie turned to Jolene, but she looked away without defending him. He jerked his arm from her grip, then pointed a finger at Gristel. "Hold on here. No one's taking me off like this. Now you look, you goddamn Mister Fancy Dan; I came in here like an honest man."

Gristel snorted a laugh through his nose.

"Yeah," Artie told him, bobbing his head. "Honest."

"You came in here for one thing. You never had any intention of purchasing a unit. You could never afford a unit in a million years, but you wasted my time, made me go through the whole spiel. Everyone here knows what you were after."

"Are you calling me a liar?" Artie asked. He was shaking all over, he was so angry.

"Look at you," Gristel said. "Look in a mirror."

"Artie, stop this," Jolene said. She had Dandy hefted onto one hip and she gripped Artie's arm with her free hand. "I'm sorry, sir, we'll be on our way; now please, Artie, let's go."

"Nobody calls me a liar. I got money. I got stocks, that's what I got. You want to see them, huh? I'll show you."

He wrenched his arm from Jolene's grip. He couldn't look at her. Her standing right there and not even supporting him—that was half the trouble. He stared at Gristel and Gristel said, "Show me."

Artie started going through his pockets, but Gristel didn't stop him. He went through his pockets a second time, slower, pulling them inside out. He mumbled, "They must be out in the car. Or maybe my banker's got them." Gristel shook his head at Jolene and smirked. Artie didn't like this bit that they had together. "Who the hell are you to call me a liar?" Artie said. "Who owns this company? Who's in charge here?"

"Artie!" Jolene said.

"You just shut up," he said.

"That's it," she told him. "I can't take no more. I'm leaving."

Mr. William T. Gristel brushed right past Artie and walked Jolene to the door. Artie watched through the open doorway which separated the middle room from the front room as Gristel told her, "It was nice meeting you, miss. I wish you better luck with everything." He shook her hand and held it, as if they were friends, or lovers. Then he spoke close to her and handed her a small card.

Gristel returned and planted himself in front of Artie. He stood with his hands on his hips, rocking on his heels, looking down.

"I demand to speak to somebody important. I'm not going to

be treated like this. I came here in good faith," Artie said. He went on, but the madder he got, the shakier his voice became. He couldn't even yell. His voice scraped like a squeaking hinge. "I've got pull. I've got connections. I've got important friends. When I get through with you, you're going to be one sorry-assed motherfucker."

Gristel half turned toward the doorway that led into the back room. He raised one big hand and snapped his fingers. A tall man with a big belly and a bald head crossed the carpet toward them. He wore a dark suit and sunglasses and he seemed to just come out of that darkness behind the doorway, out of the air itself.

Artie squared his shoulders, flexed his hands, and tipped his head up. Small tremors ran through him and he could hardly keep still. But there was nothing to do about it. He told Gristel, "I'll let you have one more chance to apologize."

Jolene was standing outside the white station wagon, holding Dandy and kicking at the body rot that ran in wide swaths along the bottom of the car. There was a dent the size of a large dog caving in the passenger-side door. The car was covered with a thick coating of dirt. She said, "How can anyone take us seriously? And this isn't even our car. We can't even afford a junk like this." She shivered in the cold and looked up as the first scattered flakes of snow fell.

Artie was still ripped. Not just at Gristel but at the district manager for not even listening to his side of the story. The guy just pushed him out the door and threatened to call the cops. He didn't even shake Artie's hand.

"Get into the goddamn car," he told Jolene. "Goddamn traitor. Can't even stand by me."

"Who do you think you are, Mr. Big Time?" They both slammed their doors behind them. Artie opened his and slammed it again. "We can't even afford a place like this for one week," she said. She settled Dandy in the back.

"Maybe I hold my money," Artie said, talking to the air. "I can have money. I can hide it in my bedpost. I can own things, things more important than a car. Art treasures. Jewels. Great records. I can have money. He's got no right to pass judgment. I can be a very wealthy man." He started the car. The gas gauge was on empty. He opened his hand toward her. "You got a couple bucks for gas, Jolene?"

"This is a mess," she said. "My whole life is a mess."

"Jolene," he warned her. "Jolene."

"My name's not Jolene," she said, her voice starting off angry but going quiet rapidly.

He looked at her and wondered if she was losing it. He didn't want her to forget about the money, though, so he kept his hand out. He felt demeaned, having to wait for her to come around with the cash, wait until she felt like giving it to him.

She said, "It's not Jolene, it's Janet. I thought Jolene . . ." She bent her head sideways, her eyes distant, like she was daydreaming. "It's pretty. It's different. It sounds like someone special."

"Is that true? Is that true?" he asked with sudden rising anger. The anger was so intense he wondered himself where it was coming from. But it gave him a sense of power, and he let himself flow with the building tension. He found himself saying to her, "Have you been lying to me all this time?"

"You got to do something. You got to try something. How else can you change things?"

It felt like his chest was pulling apart on him, like a mass of fury was ripping it open from the inside. Dandy began crying in the back seat and Artie yelled, "Shut up!" over his shoulder.

Dandy whimpered for a few seconds, but he went right back to his noise.

Artie turned to Jolene. "What are you trying to pull on me?" She didn't answer, just lit a cigarette, didn't answer him, and he pressed his teeth together until his gums hurt. "Don't ignore me, goddamn you. You better come across with some answers." Dandy was sobbing in loud, repeating bursts and Artie screamed, "Just shut up, Dandy!" But Dandy only started in louder. Artie put his hands to the steering wheel and pushed himself back into the seat, holding his arms taut.

"I pulled you out of a goddamned Jello-O pit and gave you the best two months of my life," he said. Dandy was wailing like a siren, and she was sitting there ignoring everything Artie said to her. But if I was her kid she wouldn't ignore me, Artie thought. Or if I was Mr. William T. goddamned Gristel with a fancy fucking suit. "Answer me, goddamn you," he demanded. But she sat there looking out the window, acting like he didn't even exist.

"Jolene," he said. Someone was watching them from behind the curtains in the building. Dandy kept crying. He just would not shut up. "Jolene," Artie said, his voice loud so he could be heard over Dandy's racket. "Jolene!" he told her. She sat there, looking away, going off by herself in her mind. His hands were trembling on the wheel, his arm muscles tight, and her kid would not stop, the noise coming like a toothache. The world turned purple, and Artie couldn't help himself.

"You goddamned little shit!" he yelled, the words bursting from his mouth. He whirled and in one motion whacked Dandy across the face with the back of his hand. There was a loud crack, and Dandy's glasses fell off and fell into the space between the door and the seat.

What have I done? Artie thought. But he didn't have time to think it through because Jolene, Janet, he didn't know anymore, started screeching. "You no-good bastard!" She threw her fists at him until he had to smack her too, to get her to stop, but with his open hand, so it wouldn't show or hurt so much. She touched her fingers to where he'd hit her on the cheek and her eyes opened and the tears came. Artie stared at his hand as if it would speak to him.

She wiggled over into the back seat to be with her boy and Artie was alone. He was so confused. But he had had enough of this no-money shit. He needed cash. At least the feel of a few dollars in his pocket. He thought of the Wrangler. She'd done it before. It wasn't that bad. There was something else in his mind, though. A kind of sentimental feeling, not wanting other men to see her or say things to her. But money's money, he told himself, and he pushed those soft feelings away so he wouldn't have to think about them.

He gripped the steering wheel and stared at the wooden building, at the sign and the photographs. She was saying something in the back seat, mumbling something soothing and apologetic to Dandy . What about me? What about my feelings? Artie thought, but he didn't say anything. He figured if he let it go, it'd all blow over.

Then he started thinking about deceit: it was all around him, going on all over the world, everywhere, making it hard for a man to get ahead.

He looked in the rearview mirror and angled it down until he saw her reflection. She was bent across Dandy, retrieving his glasses from beside the seat. Artie pointed his finger at that image. "You know," he said and he nodded his head. "Someday . . ."

She looked up at his eyes in the mirror and moved even closer to Dandy, protecting him with the circle of her arms. She punched out her words at Artie. "Someday what?"

He didn't know what to say next. The violence of her question shot through his mind, clearing out his thoughts. Finally he told her, "Someday I'll be gone and then . . ." And then what?

"It don't matter nothing whether you're gone or whether you stay," she said. He closed his lips to cover his teeth. After a minute he started to hum, then to whistle. He cranked up the car, still whistling, backed it up, and turned it forward onto the street.

"I don't even want you around anymore," Jolene told him. "So when we get home you can just pack up your things and get out. All your talk, and you haven't brought me nothing lately but grief."

It was snowing hard now, large heavy flakes that would freeze as night came on and the temperature dropped. He pulled on his headlights and they spread a dim yellow sheen onto the roadway for a few feet in front of the car; then the light seemed to evaporate. In the distance the road tapered off and it was all white, the sky completely blank. The trees running forward along both sides of his vision crouched beside the road like dark, shaggy animals rolled into themselves for protection and warmth.

He stared down the long, empty stretch of road before him and cut through the silence inside the car with his keening whistle. It was going to be an awful long ride home, he thought, but he was thankful for the time. It would give him a chance to think.

He leaned forward to see better; then he stamped his foot on the button on the floor. But the high beams were broken, or the switch was, and he peered forward nervously, just barely able to see a snatch of the way before him through the rapidly thickening snow.

# CHAPTER
# —7—

It started with a chugging sound; then the engine began skipping and the station wagon shook so violently that Artie could barely keep his hands on the wheel.

"Come on, you bitch." He pounded his hand once on the dashboard. As if he expected the car to be able to see what he could, he pointed out the front window. Half a mile ahead the road curved uphill onto a dull silver bridge, which arced to a point in the sky where it seemed to dissolve into the storm. "You can make it that goddamned far," Artie said.

The car rattled more violently and slowed, losing power, even though he kept the gas pedal clamped to the floor. Smoke began pouring from the cracks in the hood. The car gave one last lurching heave and shudder. Then it died. They were in the passing lane.

"See? See what you did? You and your bad luck, bringing it down on us," Artie said. He moved the rearview mirror so he could see Jolene better. He hoped she felt guilty. She didn't look so mad anymore, just disgusted. When she didn't argue back he thought maybe things were looking up. Maybe he was getting through to her.

"Shouldn't you have pulled over into the breakdown lane?" she asked. "This is a breakdown, isn't it?"

"Jolene, now darling, honey, we've got enough troubles. Let's not be at each other." He smiled over his shoulder but she lowered her eyes. "I figured if I stayed in the passing lane the car would get the idea and pick up on the speed, you know? You know how cars are sometimes. Sensitive. Just like me." The smoke was rolling so heavily out of the engine that it looked like a small cloud had covered the front of the car. "Come on now, gal, give me a hand pushing it over and we'll get us some help."

"What for? Why should I help you? I been thinking a lot, sitting in this car."

"Now don't let yourself start thinking," he said. "Talk about trouble. Look, we had this little unimportant disagreement. You think Romeo and Juliet didn't yap at each other sometimes?"

"You used physical force," she said.

"Hey gal, look, I'm sorry. Okay? But you weren't helping me none."

"When was the last time you helped me with anything?"

He turned forward. He could feel her eyes, wanting him to look at her. No way was that going to happen. He watched the smoke climb the hood and spread along the windshield. It rolled on the glass as if it wanted to get in, then drifted in loose patches down both sides of the car, poking at the doors.

After a minute he saw two cars approaching in the passenger-side mirror. He fixed the interior mirror and spoke to her in it. "We don't want little Dandy to get smashed up in some accident, do we?" He watched her face as the cars passed them on the right. The second car let out a stream of noise from its horn. Artie sounded out a response with his, but there was still so much smoke on the windshield that he couldn't see the driver's reaction.

"You're right," Jolene said, smiling at him like she got the joke. She glanced behind them, where the highway stretched in a straight line. The snow seemed not to fall so much as to swirl in the air back there. The tar was covered with a thin sheet of white cut through by the tire marks from the cars that had just passed. She cracked the handle on her door.

"That's my gal," Artie said. "See? We can work together, Jolene. I'm telling you, no one's going to beat us, the two of us together." He wanted to tell her he was sorry for hitting her and, yeah, for hitting the kid too. If he could, he'd take it all back; he'd do things differently. How could he tell her, though, without it seeming like he was apologizing and being weak? He decided it was enough that he thought about it—good intentions and all—so he said nothing, just opened his door and stepped out.

He placed one foot on the grassy partition separating the north and south lanes, then leaned in the window he had rolled down and grabbed the steering wheel with both hands. He was just able to hold on and keep his head out, lean it on the doorframe, so he could see the road. "Let me know when you're ready and I'll shift into neutral," he called. Her door slammed and he smiled. A love song burst into his mind. He whistled it to her. After a few seconds he said, "Ready? Jolene? Here goes now, get set." He shifted the stick on the column and the car pulled backward on him. "Whoa," he called and moved his feet quickly so he wouldn't fall. He slipped a bit at first, but he finally got his boots dug in. He had to put all his strength and weight into it just to hold the car steady. "Come on, goddamn, put your back into it."

Then he saw her crossing to the other side of the road, walking backward up ahead of him. She was heading toward the bridge, moving fast. She held Dandy with her left hand, half-lifting, half-dragging the kid so his feet just scraped the road. Her right hand was loose, like it was ready to come up to thumb a ride. The buttons were gone on her coat, and it flared open to show her white cotton button-down shirt.

"What the hell you doing?" he yelled.

"I'm going home. *My* home."

"What about me?" A car slowed as it moved between them and the driver looked over at Artie. "Get the fuck out of here," Artie yelled. The driver snapped forward and the car fishtailed off through the snow. Jolene hefted Dandy onto her hip and turned around. She started in with those long strides of hers, heading away.

Artie let go of the wheel and stepped back. He set his hands on his hips. This was a new one. How could she just walk off like that, he thought. Turn her back on everything they'd been building together. He had a brief impression that he was moving; then he realized it was the car, rolling away. Goddamn me, he thought. Things moving off in different directions and I'm just standing here, not knowing which way to go.

There was really no choice. Besides, it was pretty level, where they'd come from, so the car wouldn't roll too far. It wasn't his car either. Never would be. And Smitty wouldn't ever put him up for more than a night.

He had to run to catch up to her. Twice he slipped and stumbled and caught himself with his hands to the tar before he fell flat. His chest was heaving and drool seeped from the corners of his mouth. He wiped it off with his sleeve, then focused on her back, watched it grow larger. Now he was close enough to touch her. Her head started to turn toward him and he grabbed her shoulder and spun her around. "Now come on now, what are you doing to me?" he asked, the words coming out on his panting breath.

"Come on nothing," she told him, windmilling her arm to throw his hand off. She saw a car in the distance, coming at them, and she hopped backward and thrust her thumb out. She craned her neck to try to catch the driver's eye. Snow covered her hair like a lace veil.

"This ain't funny no more," he said. He stepped forward and pulled her arm down.

She ripped her arm away from him. "Neither is hitting me," she said. "Neither is hitting my baby."

"Jesus Christ, I already apologized," he said, but she was walking backward, staring at him, trying to nail him where he stood with the violent hammer of her look.

Artie made a lunge for the kid. He figured, if he could get ahold of Dandy, she'd have to come with him. He missed and his hand caught the pocket of her shirt, just above her breast. She wrenched backward, but he held on, moving with her.

She jerked herself sharply from side to side, snapping her body like a fish trying to throw a hook. Buttons popped. They curved upward into the air, then pattered softly into the snow by their feet. He held on as she stumbled backward, splaying her legs to find her balance point. Her buttons were all ripped loose now, and she clawed at the hand in her pocket. Then she formed a fist and backhanded him in the mouth.

He let go and brought both hands to his face. He touched his lips, holding his fingers to them as if reading a message. When he lowered his hands and looked at the blood on his fingers he cried, "What are you doing to me?" His voice was a squeal. He felt weak and dizzy, on the edge of a faint, and he touched his mouth again.

Her face shone as if lit internally by a dark light and she ran sideways, holding her hand out and waving it. She carried Dandy like a sack under her other arm, and Artie could see her breast flopping out of her shirt. Jealousy perked up inside him, even as he wished briefly that she'd fall and slip under the tires of the small brown car that puttered to a halt beside her. She wrenched open the door and pushed and angled her body into the interior, cramming herself in. It took him a second to realize what was happening; then he was moving fast, closing the gap between them.

He grabbed at the handle just as he heard the click of the lock. He swore he could still feel her warmth in the air around him.

"Let me in! Open up, goddamn you. Jolene?" He slammed his palm on the window. The glass rattled. When he pulled his hand away there were fingerprints of blood on the glass. He lowered his face and looked past Jolene to the driver, a man with a soft, frightened, round face. Artie set his bloodied hand on the window and called, "It's your blood if you don't let me in this fucking car."

He grabbed at the handle again, yanked it up, then kicked the door, as if he thought it might pop open. He watched Jolene's head turn toward the driver and he heard her strident orders: "Get moving, get moving, hurry up, get the hell out of here." The little car spun its wheels, then sputtered ahead. Artie ran with it, holding onto the handle, banging on the window, yelling, "Stop! Stop! I'm warning you. It's your blood. You'll pay for this. You'll fucking pay!" The car gathered speed and hit the base of the bridge, and Artie had to let go. He slowed to a walk and listened to the loud vibrating of his heart. His mouth opened into a circle as he took in air, then his lips pulled into a grimace as the coldness hit his lungs. He looked hard at the back of the car to memorize the license plate. The man's face was already a permanent detail in his mind.

The car became a speck as it moved up to the crest of the bridge; then it, too, dissolved with the girders into the solid swirl of the storm.

He stood for some seconds, watching the empty road rise before him, seeing it through a confetti of snow that fell like the debris from an explosion. He almost expected to see the car drive back down the hill and stop for him. He'd get inside and they'd all be friends, laughing and joking. He looked down to see his feet covered with snow.

He'd been in some jams in his life—left out, tossed out—in situations where people refused to make a place for him. But this might be the worst he'd ever faced. He stood staring up the bridge; he hoped Jolene had at least covered up her breast. Then he understood for the first time that he had been hoping that somehow this thing with Jolene would be it. Somehow it would last, and she'd help him get out of the life he was in and into one that was better. Why hadn't he seen that before? How had things gone bad?

It took a while for the cold to inform his senses, but it came to him, as he stood watching the snow pile on his feet, that he was shivering. He took one last look at the empty bridge before he started back to the car at a run.

The wagon had lodged its back end into a steel pole in the railing running the length of the median strip. The front end of the car jutted into the passing lane. Artie sat inside, but it gave him no protection from the cold. He felt strained from all the running he'd done. Sharp pains jabbed through his chest. His mind floated somewhere above his body. It took him some time to catch his breath, and when he finally did he tried the key. The starter made a clicking noise.

He gripped tight to the steering wheel and yanked himself

forward into the windshield. "Jolene," he called, smashing himself into the glass. The word had come unbidden and when he pulled himself forward a second time he found himself yelling "You!" He kept it up, "Jolene!" "You!" the smashing, until he felt his forehead become soft and numb. The skin cracked open and blood seeped out. With one final surge he threw himself forward. A small fissure opened in the glass and he leaned back, dazed, uncertain of his thoughts. He allowed himself a brief, bitter smile, then he slumped down in his seat and closed his eyes, thinking he was a pretty damn poor excuse for a human being.

He heard the sound of a car engine and the squeal of brakes in the same instant and looked to the right behind him. A Volkswagen skidded full speed toward him. The driver's face was just visible: a young girl, her mouth open in terror. She looked at Artie as if she expected him to somehow stop this, do something. The last thing he thought before the cars collided was—whiplash, lawsuit, money. Then he felt the jar of contact, and the tearing metal noise and waterlike sound of breaking glass splintered in his ears.

# CHAPTER

# —8—

With Dandy's birth, Jolene had been convinced things would get better for her. How could they not? Her checks and food stamps would give them enough money to get by on, and now there'd be two of them. But somehow just getting by didn't seem enough, and even with a baby there she was still lonely most of the time. She'd run into a few men along the way, but they were always temporaries. They only seemed concerned with taking care of their own needs and some of them even stole things from her, odd things, like silverware or tubes of lipstick. None of them were interested in working on something lasting. Which was fine with her, since she hadn't really liked any of them all that much to begin with.

She hadn't really gone with anyone until Artie had come along two months ago. That was the longest she'd ever been with a guy, and though he wasn't perfect, she'd had hopes for him. Even when he sat around drinking all day he'd made her laugh. That was something, wasn't it? If someone acted like that, weren't they trying to keep you happy? And it was like he really enjoyed being with her, too, and not just in bed. But today, in the car, when he turned and hit Dandy, she felt inside just as she had when her father had visited her bedroom—something was starting that she couldn't control. She experienced a terror similar to the one she'd known when she was six and had seen her father naked for the first time, standing on the threshold of her room, asking if she was Daddy's girl. She hadn't known then what was going to happen, but her chest had tightened and her heart beat so loudly it felt like it was on the surface of her skin. Her father limped across the room and spread her legs like a wishbone.

She screamed with the pain and he covered her face with a pillow, then yelled at her for bleeding and for being a little tramp, a goddamned whore, and if she said one word, just *one,* goddamn it, he'd toss her ass out into the street and have the police arrest her.

Jolene's hands were shaking now, and she put them under her legs. There was no sense going over that, she told herself. No sense remembering things that had happened and couldn't be changed. She forced herself back to the present, to her situation. Artie.

When he'd hit her, she couldn't help thinking about what she'd been through with Henry. Was it starting all over again? she wondered. How could she have been so wrong about everything?

It wasn't only Artie that upset her, though. Before he blew up she'd been wondering what life would've been like if she had had an abortion. Artie's actions seemed somehow connected to her own thoughts. She wondered if she were to blame, if her thinking harm on her baby made Artie hit Dandy because Artie was so tuned in to her and just wanted her to be happy. She knew it sounded crazy, but she couldn't shake the idea. Maybe she deserved to be hit. Maybe she deserved everything that had happened to her.

When the car broke down in the snowstorm, she saw it as a chance for her to get away, have time to think. If she could get to the apartment before him, she could straighten it all out in her mind and plan what to do next. "I just need to be alone," she said.

"Excuse me?" a man's voice said. "Are you all right?"

She turned to the voice, blinking to clear off the memories and bring herself back to the present. It took a second to remember where she was, who the man was, and to understand that the weight in her lap was her baby sleeping.

She lifted Dandy gently, leaned through the opening between the front seats, and placed him on the floor in the back. It'd be safer that way; he couldn't roll over and fall off anywhere.

Turning around, she caught the man smiling at her. She smiled back but he looked ahead quickly. She glanced down and saw that her right breast was completely exposed. She laughed. "Looks like I'm going to need some buttons." She saw once again the buttons popping off one by one as Artie pulled on her shirt, trying to get her to stay, and she felt uncertain about her leaving.

The man watched out of the corner of his eye as she tucked her breast inside her shirt and pulled her coat over to cover herself. Something about his appearance reminded her of a turtle: his square bald head, his overbite. A turtle with thick-framed glasses.

"Well," she said. "How far can you take us?" She looked at the snow, whipping down heavily and collecting on the road. It was so deep she could almost feel its pull dragging on the car.

He motioned in front of him with a hand covered by a tan leather driving glove. His eyes lit up like a child's with a present. "I'll take you as far as you want to go."

"You don't know how much this means to me," Jolene said. "How can I ever thank you?"

"Well." The man chuckled, facing forward in his seat. He moved himself back and forth as if digging in backward. He raised his eyebrows at his own thoughts and let a smile slice open his mouth. From the left-hand pocket of his sports coat he removed a dark brown pipe with a black handle and set it in his mouth without lighting it.

She looked past him, at the houses on his side of the road. She couldn't see their edges. They were barely visible, snugged into themselves against the furious whirl of the storm, defined by the yellow glow of their windows, like bright patches stitched into the landscape. She looked at the man; his face was without a beard shadow, but its overall roundness was broken by small sunken areas along his jawline where it looked like parts of him were collapsing inward. It reminded Jolene of her father, a big man whose flesh was pushed in in odd places on his body, so that he gave the impression of being hollow and dented.

She shivered and shook the images away. This man was something regular. You could tell he had a real life, a real job, a real family. "Do you—I mean, you must have a house, right?"

"Of course I have a house. I'm a grown man," he said, as if telling a joke. But there was a nervousness in his voice, like he was thinking about something else and didn't want her to find out what it was.

"That's something," she told him, looking at her lap. The material of her pants was worn down so that the area above her knees was slick and shiny. "Is it big? Is it—"

"It's nothing extravagant. Your basic split-level. Three bedrooms, one and a half baths."

"How did you get it? I mean—" She felt stupid, not even knowing how to ask the questions right. "I don't understand how people get there. I mean, you had to go through something, right? College or something?"

The man looked at her intensely, to make sure she wasn't joking. His eyes descended from her face. She looked at herself and pulled her shirt closed with one hand. When she looked back at him he was rigid, watching the road. He felt her eyes on him and removed the pipe from his mouth. "Yes—um, I have a graduate degree, I'm an engineer. It's—uh, lucrative. . . . I have a house, a small boat . . . pretty much everything I desire." He glanced at her. "I guess you can view it as a continuum. You begin at a certain point and work on. I'm at the point now where I can pay for anything I want. Within reason, of course." He gripped the pipe tightly with his teeth, then slowly closed his lips on the stem.

"Is there something going on here I'm missing?" she asked. He laughed and winked at her. She felt like something was floating around above her head, but she put that aside and thought about the man's position. "What if you never get to the first point? What if you never even get that far?"

"You're young. And sexy," he said, voicing the word breathily, as if he'd never said it aloud before.

She gave him a questioning glance and he looked embarrassed. He moved the pipe from the far to the near side of his mouth.

"Everyone gets to some point," he said, the words falling flat in the close interior.

She shook her head. "I don't know about that." She stared at the holes in the ceiling. "I'd give anything just to have something—maybe just to have a little money I could be saving for something."The words popped out of her mouth like bubbles.

"Peek-a-boo," he said.

"What's that supposed to mean?"

He pointed at her with his pipe stem. "You'll freeze to death."

She pulled her shirt together again with one hand and waved the other vaguely at the windshield. That was the least of her worries, she thought, looking at the snow. Then her mind cracked open onto the realization that this man had, indeed, saved their lives. If it wasn't for him, she and Dandy would be out on the road, frozen over like snowmen. That unsettled her. She'd never really felt that she could, in fact, die. Or that Dandy could, either. "You really did save me and my baby," she said. "How can I ever thank you?"

"We'll work out something." His voice was taut, high-pitched.

She leaned her head on the side window to think, to figure out what was happening here. The snow was melting on the glass. She jumped back; Artie's bloody fingerprints were still visible on the outside of the glass, the whorls and lines blurred, the blood streaking in pale rose streams down the window.

"Is something wrong?" the driver asked.

She looked ahead at the yellow from the headlights. The beams illuminated the snow in a small square patch. It was like they were following a movie screen that kept moving forward with them. She shook her head and said, "No." She gave him a weak smile. Tearing her eyes away from him in order to watch the road, she added, "Nothing at all," and then it came tumbling down on her. "Only my whole damn life."

He fidgeted with the steering wheel, glanced at her, then locked his head forward, toward the road. He held his pipe contemplatively in his left hand and opened his mouth three times, as if to say something, but only ran his tongue modestly across his lips. "Maybe I can help," he said finally.

Before she could reply he snapped on the radio full volume. The soft sounds of strings and woodwinds filled the car, so loud she had to cover her ears. He fiddled the volume all the way down, eased it up to a comfortable level, then moved the station selector bar until he found a rock-and-roll song.

She sat there for a while, very still, hands to her head, her thoughts as flurried and unfocused as the snow in front of them. She couldn't really be sure he said, "I just got paid," because when she looked at him he was gazing straight ahead, watching the road, both hands firmly on the wheel, his suit coat neat, his cheeks clean-shaven, looking every bit the man of responsibility.

# CHAPTER

# —9—

It was warmer in the city, and the snow was mostly slush. He followed her up the three flights of stairs. The bulb was gone from the socket outside her door and they felt their way up the last flight, pulling on the shaky banister as if it were a safety rope. His hand covered hers briefly, but he removed it before she could even turn around.

"Sit down," she told him. She lowered Dandy to the floor and pushed up the temperature on the gas log on the side of the stove. The man sat in the chair at the far end of the table, closest to the door. He unbuttoned his suede coat and fluffed the fleece collar with his fingers. He picked fibers off his suit jacket.

"Do you have any coffee?" he asked.

She opened the cupboard above the stove. There was a jar of peanut butter, a package of saltines, a stack of ketchup packets, some loose dispenser napkins, and a small corner's worth of dishes; a few plates, two mugs, and a handful of silverware. She put the peanut butter on the table and took down the mugs. One had a drawing of Snoopy on it, the other was busy with penguins performing a variety of sexual acts.

"Oh, damn," she said, and dumped a dead roach from the Snoopy mug into the paper shopping bag set against the wall between the refrigerator and the bathroom door.

She put the mugs on the table and he looked inside them. He turned the Snoopy mug over and an antenna fell out. "Well, we don't have coffee anyways," Jolene said, smiling. She brushed the antenna onto the floor. "I'm sorry."

"Juice will be fine," he told her, looking directly at her for the first time. His lips were tight and his blue eyes hard and cloudy. When he smiled, the dents in his face enlarged.

On the top shelf of the refrigerator were a stick of margarine and a quart bottle of Pepsi. There was a jar of mustard behind the margarine. "I feel like Mother Hubbard," she said, and she took out the Pepsi bottle and shook it at him. The bottle was nearly empty. "I'd give you some, but it's all I got left for my baby's bottle."

"You give that to your child?"

"Well, you can't expect me to give him coffee."

He nodded his head, smirked, and took off his coat, shaking it once briskly, as if he were checking for life, before he hung it on the back of his chair. His fingers shook and he reached inside the inner pocket of his gray tweed suit coat. He pulled out a wallet and dropped it on the table, then pushed back in his chair. He looked at the wallet. His features opened wide, like an adult acting up for a child. He caught her eye, wanting her to notice what was on the table, to have her confirm it. The way his head yearned toward her she knew he wanted her to speak. But what was she supposed to say? Jolene stepped back from the table, keeping her eyes on him. He sat back and took his pipe from his pocket, cupping it in his hands briefly before raising it to his mouth. When he spoke he looked away, at Dandy, who was lying on his stomach in front of the stove, moving his head from side to side and grunting softly.

"I just cashed my paycheck." He spoke quietly, like a man trying not to admit something. His voice was shaky and his fingers trembled on the tabletop. His legs wavered back and forth, opening and shutting beneath the table with a soft flapping sound. He poked at the wallet with one hand, moved the tips of his fingers slowly in and out of the bill flap, then thrust them all the way in, up to his knuckles, all the time making a clicking noise with his mouth, like a man calming a horse. He moved his hand around inside the wallet, then pulled out a flared deck of tens and twenties.

The refrigerator was still open behind her, and she felt the cold waving up her back. The light from inside spread her shadow across the wooden floor, the tabletop, and up the wall between the windows. The shadow stretched in a long, thin, widening patch, but with the light from the overhead it was more an outline of darkness than a deep shadow. The freezer's running sounds, which always reminded her of insects, filled her head. She watched the sweat form in a line at the top of the man's forehead. He picked up a crumpled napkin from the table, searched it for a clean corner, and patted his skin dry. The sweat re-formed immediately. She looked at Dandy, then over to his box, then up at the cupboard, its door still open.

She put the Pepsi on the top shelf, the margarine on the second, and the mustard on the bottom, trying to make the refrigerator look fuller. The door made a heavy, thumping click as she shut it. She could kill Artie, she could kill herself for letting him take the last of her money for gas. Why did she have to be faced with this? She leaned against the refrigerator and propped her chin on the top of the door. "And you're just going to leave afterward." The sentence sounded like a half-question, half-request. She wasn't sure herself how she meant it.

She waited, but he didn't reply. She turned to face him.

He looked at her and shook his head and held his arms out. His mouth was open, but it didn't look like he wanted to talk. Maybe he wanted something to eat. He stood up and babbled without making a full sentence out of any of the words. She heard none of it. She was thinking about the ride, the money.

"What do you want from me?" she screamed. "What the hell do all of you want from me? Jesus H. Christ!" She grabbed the sides of her head to keep it from breaking apart.

He began rubbing the collar of his coat. "If you don't need anything . . ." he said, but he didn't move.

After a while she told him, "No."

She stepped to the table and snatched up the wallet. Jolene, Jolene, what are you getting into? she asked herself. Her bottom lip was quivering and she had to hold it between her teeth to make it stop. With quick resolve she pulled two twenties from the billfold. Holding them aloft, flaglike, she dropped the wallet to the table. A mindless calm settled over her.

She swept Dandy off the floor and kissed him on the lips. He shook his head and pushed his tongue out. Drool fell onto her open shirt and she let it sit there. She rubbed the bills over his head, then placed him in his box, covering him with the bath towel she used as his blanket. She slipped the twenties under his small throw pillow, then took off his glasses and left them on the table.

When Jolene turned her attention to him, the man began to talk. He looked at the table as he spoke. His voice firmed, took on an edge, but she could sense he was still nervous. He told her how excited she made him, how he had never felt this way before, how he wanted to make this a weekly thing, blah blah blah. She believed none of it. She wasn't required to. She wasn't even required to listen.

She drifted into the other room and stripped off her clothing. "C'mon," she yelled. When he entered he stopped abruptly, like a fighter walking forward into a punch. He looked around the room. His arms circled in on himself, as if for protection from what he saw, the bleakness and the mess. Slowly he began to undress. Moving like a person waking up from a long sleep, he folded everything neatly, placing it in a small pile on the floor: his jacket, pants, dress shirt, boxer shorts, undershirt. He placed his socks inside his shoes in front of his clothing so that their toes pointed at the mattress, pipe nestling between them, the stem thrusting up. Only when he was naked did he look at Jolene. She lay there, her legs spread, twisting a hank of hair on the side of her head. He stepped onto the mattress and stood by her feet.

"How do I compare?" he said, "I mean, I'm above average, aren't I?"

"I've never done anything like this." She didn't look at him.

"Sure," he said.

He hesitated for a minute, then told her, "Put it in your mouth." She sat up mechanically and walked on her knees to where he stood at the edge of the mattress. She saw only his half-erect penis, the tan cap rimmed with purple, the slate-blue slit she thought of as the eye. She halted before it and stared.

"Put it in," he said with urgency, grabbing her awkwardly, roughly, by the hair on the back of her head.

Yes, Daddy, she thought, cracking her mouth wide and leaning forward.

It had gone on and on with him. Every time her mother was out, he'd come in and make her kneel on the bed. He stood with his hands on his hips and made her work until her mouth was so sore she couldn't help crying. Then he'd push her flat and ram into her so hard her head often banged against the wall.

She began to feel like she wasn't there when it happened, like she was someone else, and that feeling enveloped her until the day at school when she walked to the middle of the playground at recess and lifted her dress to show everyone she didn't have any panties on. Soon there was a circle around her, boys and girls, watching her finger herself while she yelled all the swears she could think of.

When her teacher came running across the tarred playground, Janet opened her arms and made grasping motions with her hands. But the teacher just pushed down Janet's skirt and pointed the way to the nurse's office.

She sat alone in the waiting room while the nurse and the principal spoke with her mother and father, who'd been called in, and she listened to the muffled voices, scared and outraged, and then to the absolute silence.

In the car on the way home she tried to tell them. Over and over she swore she hadn't told anyone anything, not one word. They acted like she wasn't talking, like she wasn't even there, and she curled up in a ball on the floor and wished that she could die.

She was sick for a long time after that, constant severe stomach cramps and diarrhea, but no one even spoke with her, except for the woman from Social Services, who visited once a week for six months until, she told Janet, it was clear everything was going to be all right.

Of course, the story of the playground followed her through every grade. She never had boyfriends, and the girls weren't allowed to play with her. Soon, those situations started, those times when she just lost control.

She stared at the ceiling. She just wasn't smart enough to understand her own self, she guessed. Was anybody? She had those same mixed-up feelings inside her now that she had after those "amnesia" times—that she hadn't really done anything, but she was still somehow to blame for what had happened. And then there was the other feeling—that there might be a way to escape all this, if she only knew how.

He dressed with his back to her, talking the whole time, telling her he'd be back soon. They could set up a weekly schedule. She knew he had to be just talking. He couldn't mean it. She wanted to tell him to forget it, he didn't have to pretend, it had been her decision. But that seemed too complicated a thing to explain. He named a day and she told him, Sure, that was fine, her calendar was open. She didn't even have a calendar. A crampy feeling started in her stomach, like she was going to have the runs, and she propped herself up on her arms and watched him, hoping he'd hurry up and leave.

He brushed all the dust from his jacket and straightened it neatly on his frame. His back was to her. He said, "It doesn't really matter, it doesn't make any difference, I don't really care, I just need to know, just in case, my wife and all—are there any, do you have any . . . diseases I should be aware of? I don't mind, I just need to know."

She felt like she was being frozen, the cold shrinking her body, pressing it into a tiny cube. She wanted to yell and scream at him, throw things, something. But in that pause when she tried to figure out exactly what to do, what to say, she realized she didn't even know his name. She saw herself as he must—a woman willing to suck a stranger's cock for money. She didn't know where to begin to explain it to him, to tell him it wasn't the way it seemed, it wasn't so simple. So she said nothing. She lay there. It felt like things were breaking off inside her chest and falling, but never landing anywhere.

She stayed in the bedroom until she heard the door shut. Wrapping a blanket around herself, she walked into the kitchen. The floor was cold and she tried to step without putting her feet flat, just walking on the edges. The blanket covered her just past her waist; cool and warm air crawled up her legs and ass in contending currents.

She stepped to the window, to see what was with the snow, and to try to see the man's car as he drove down the small patch of road visible between her building and the one across the way.

But her eyes never made it outside. On the top sill of the bottom window, lined up, sitting, standing, begging, curled as if for sleep, were Artie's dogs: shepherd, collie, terrier, poodle, hound. They were opalescent on the sill; they glowed faintly as if they contained radiant centers. She lifted the shepherd. *The Lord is my shepherd,* she thought, but she knew that wasn't true. The dog's mouth was open, the teeth and tongue finely detailed, and she put it back on the sill quickly. She was afraid that through some act of will Artie might be able to bring it to life and have it attack her. She knew that wasn't really possible. But still.

She turned and looked on the table for the money. The man's money. Her money. Dandy made a choking sound and she swung around to him. He was thrashing in his box, as if he couldn't breathe.

"My baby!" Jolene cried. She pulled him out of the box and dug her fingers into his mouth. Something soft was wadded at the back of his throat. He was jerking in her arms and she pushed it deeper when she tried to close her fingers around it. She turned him upside down, held his ankles, and shook him hard. Nothing fell out. She turned him around again, held his jaw open with one hand, and was just able to stretch one finger down deep enough to scratch up the obstruction. It was a ball of paper made from the ripped-up, chewed-together pieces of a twenty-dollar bill. Dandy was crying and hiccoughing.

"Oh no, oh no, oh no," Jolene said in a singsong voice. She began shaking him, gently at first, then harder. "Do you know what I had to do for that? Do you have any idea?" Her voice rose to a scream. "What are you doing? What are you doing to me?" She held him by his sides and shook him so violently he snapped about like he was jointless. He was crying so hard his face was a tight scarlet ball.

She felt her face take on the attitude of her mother's—the teeth chopping air as she screamed, the nose flaring open. Even the words echoed what her mother had said that day she came home from her shift at Woolworth's to find her daughter sobbing on a blood-spotted mattress. She had grabbed Jolene by the arms and jostled her as if trying to shake dust out of her pores. "What are you doing to me?" she said, the cigarette bouncing in the corner of her mouth and dropping its ash to the bed. Then, softer, her mother asked, "So you're a big girl now, huh? You think you're a regular Shirley Temple, don't you?" She left the room and returned a minute later with an iron in her hand. Without a word, she jabbed it onto her daughter's stomach, burning a sickle-shaped scar into the flesh.

Jolene dropped Dandy suddenly and was just able to catch him by one arm before he hit the floor. She wasn't going to be that kind of mother, she told herself as she lifted him to her shoulder. "Mama's sorry, honey. She's so sorry." She kissed his head and patted his back until he calmed down. She hugged Dandy closer and looked at a dog on the windowsill, its tongue hanging out between sharp pointed teeth, its ears erect, alert; the whole thing gleaming. She thought, Artie and me, we're just the same. Maybe we deserved each other.

# CHAPTER —10—

She passed the night in squalls of sleep, dozing off for a few violent minutes every so often, then thrashing awake and reaching over for Artie. She was surprised that she missed him, and she worried about where he was and what he was doing. She hoped to God he hadn't died. How can you even think that? she scolded herself. Still, where was he? And if something happened to him, wouldn't it be her fault? She slid into a sleep where maimed dogs—legless shepherds and poodles with their skulls split open—stalked her over a charred, smoking earth.

Once it was the rattle of Artie's sleeping breaths, the disturbed nightmare gasps he always took, that woke her. She sat up, sweating in the cold air, and tried to find him through the darkness and the fog coming from her mouth. Finally she flicked on the light. All she saw were the scattered pieces of his clothing, like discarded hopes.

The certainty of his presence was so strong it felt like a hook had been set into her lungs. She stood on the mattress in the light and turned in a circle. There was something in the corner to her left. She bent down to see. Two pewter dogs stood back end to back end at the intersection of the wall.

She stood up quickly and shivered. In the next corner there were two dogs as well, and two in the corner by the closet. She wondered how she could've missed seeing them before, but she knew she wasn't one to look closely at what was around her in her life. The corner by the door was empty, as were the corners in the kitchen, though in that room the dogs lined the windowsills.

She felt she had to find all the dogs, so she searched everywhere. Two collies sat like sentinels on either side of the toilet bowl. Another dog guarded the top shelf of the empty medicine cabinet.

She felt like she'd been violated, as if she were the object of a complex curse, voodoo or something. She wanted to crawl under the blanket and let somebody else find out what was going on. But she knew nobody was going to do it for her. She walked along the walls, her hands touching them; her eyes scoured the floor. She halted at the closet.

The far door was open and she could see nothing but her clothes spilling onto the floor. She put her hands to the other door, the one that closed off Artie's side, and shoved it down its runner.

Hanging from the bar by a noose of twined fiber was a crude cross of broken planking. It was nailed together and painted black, the arms splintered on the ends into pointing fingers. The head of a stuffed dog covered the top shaft, held in place by the noose around its neck. The tongue of the dog, a bright red, lolled out of its brown snout.

Her mind slid into a low-level state of shock and she couldn't move. She shivered uncontrollably. She stared at the cross; it was some time before she could tear her eyes away. On the floor was the rest of Artie's collection; deep in the corner, circling in on itself, coiled like a serpent.

The inner coils began with dogs stretched prone, heads touching tails, as if they were one continuous, segmented entity. This section curled out where the dogs took on sitting positions. When those were used up, the standing dogs finished off. They were arranged smallest to largest in each position, so the curves seemed to widen, then narrow again. Jolene, kneeling now, looked at the cross; something about the dog's head reminded her of Artie— the way the face came to a point, or maybe the look in the eyes, like it wasn't quite sure what was happening to it.

She crawled on her hands and knees to the mattress and hid under the blanket. Vague sounds of movement came to her and she whipped the blanket off her face. But the dogs in the corners of the room hadn't shifted. Though the closet door was open, the ones on the floor were too deep into the recess for her to see them. She could just make out the cross. It swung gently.

She stared for a long time, thinking of Superman and his X-ray vision, telling herself that if she really concentrated she'd be able to see through walls. There was no limit to the powers of the human mind. But the taste of sperm was still heavy in her mouth, even though she had brushed her teeth, and she knew she was being stupid. She'd never be a superhero.

What was she supposed to do? Was this a spell or something? She was afraid to look in the closet again, for fear that some weird ritual might be going on and they'd suck her inside and close the door so she couldn't get out. She thought about it some. "The only weird ritual," she told herself, "is in your brain." She watched the cross swing in and out of the light from the overhead. Something about that dog's face definitely reminded her of Artie.

Jolene looked at the flat felt eye, a black half circle inside a white oval, glued to the worn fabric of the face. The eye seemed to be looking at Jolene for help, or at least an explanation. "Oh, Artie," she said, shaking her head, thinking about how she could laugh at things that had happened, how she had memories she could feel good about. But there wasn't anything happening now for her to laugh about. That was all in the past. If he wasn't back by now, she knew he wasn't coming. She began to cry.

In the morning, with the sun steaming a bleached yellow mist through the window, things didn't seem as frightening. She missed Artie even more, though. His absence made her muscles ache like she had the flu. She hadn't realized how fully he'd become a part of her daily minutes, how much she enjoyed just having him there, how she actually looked forward to seeing his smiling face in the morning. He always woke up happy. "Why not?" he'd said when she asked him about it. "If you can make it to one more day you're ahead of the game." She knew most people wouldn't think he was any big deal. But he'd been there for her.

And if he wasn't any saint, well, she wasn't exactly the world's greatest catch either.

She gathered all the dogs and dropped them into the closet, kicking them with her foot so they fell into a loose mound in the corner. She poked with her toe to make sure none of the dogs remained upright. It wasn't that she really believed in magic, but she figured if they weren't standing the spell couldn't work anyways. She untied the noose at the bar and dropped the cross onto the pile. It didn't look scary anymore, just pathetic. Part of a game a child would play to scare himself about something he didn't understand.

She walked around the room, bent at the waist, plucking Artie's clothing from the floor. Her hand snapped each piece up, moving like a crane's head spearing food. In the pocket of a pair of dungarees he hadn't worn in some time she found a half-full pint bottle even Artie must've forgotten about. She put the whiskey on the threshold between the bedroom and the kitchen, against the doorframe. She stuffed all his things on top of the pile of miniatures, pressing down as if to smother them. That made her think of puppies and she stopped, stood up, and closed the closet door.

Dandy started crying. "What's the matter with my baby?" She changed him on the floor in the bathroom, sticking the dirty diaper in the toilet to soak, pulling down a dry one from the shower curtain bar above the bathtub. She remembered how Artie would often use the toilet anyways, claiming he'd forgotten to look, he hadn't noticed the diaper in there. That always got Jolene so mad. Now when she thought about it she felt sad. It really hadn't been such a big thing. He was just looking for attention too.

She fed Dandy some peanut butter, then filled his bottle with Pepsi mixed with water, to stretch it, and put him back in his box. "I'll let you out in a little while, honey. Mama has to clean the house." He stopped sucking on the bottle and made happy bouncing sounds with his mouth. Jolene stood back, folded her arms, and thought with amazement how her baby must really be a genius if he was already able to see how funny that was, the idea that she'd clean the house. It embarrassed her too, and she told him, "Just because I don't clean often don't mean I don't like a clean house."

On her way out to the hall for the broom and dustpan, she saw the twenty-dollar bill, the one she'd rescued, on the table. She stopped, put her fingertips to the table edge, and looked at the bill without touching it. She thought of the other bill, the one Dandy had chewed up, thinking how that about summed up how things worked. Babies and men—all they ever did was eat your money. With either one you could never get ahead. She smoothed the bill between her hands and thought of the man who'd left it. He'd been different than the men who had plagued her life. He was the type who would take care of his woman. But where was she ever going to get a chance to meet somebody like that? She remembered him walking over to kiss her forehead before he left. Like she was a little girl, she thought, and she felt suddenly childlike, defenseless. She was filled with an urge to crawl into the box with Dandy.

She stood looking at the sunlight, which slanted in the window to cut a bright bar across the back half of the table. A clarifying light filled the room. She knew a man like that would never really want someone like her. A man like that, who had nice suits and a job and a house and a . . . a wife. It was like they were from two different times, she told herself: the prehistoric and the civilized. Sure, they might each have something the other one wanted, but they'd never really fit together. Not really. She knew all this but hope still played on her heart. At first it was bitter-sweet, but soon it turned ugly in its desperation.

She swept the floors furiously with the broom, clouding the air with a dust which would only resettle, then took a facecloth and soap and scrubbed the sink and stove in the kitchen. After that she worked on the sink in the bathroom and the bathtub. She wiped the refrigerator inside and out. On hands and knees, using the same facecloth, now gone from yellow to cinder gray, she washed the bathroom floor. She was about to start on the kitchen floor, had just paused to wipe the sweat-greased hair from her forehead with the back of her hand, when an abrupt cough came from Dandy. It made her instantly aware of how quiet it was in the apartment, the silence draped like a dropcloth. She sat on her knees feeling the overwhelming presence of absence. She wanted some touch, a press of a hand to her back, her face, her breast—not for the sexuality of it but for the contact, the silent way fingers had of connecting two people, of reassuring with want. She thought of the man who had paid her, she thought of Artie, of Henry, of her father; she thought of every man and boy whom she had known. She thought of all the fingers that had touched her, all the cocks that had pressed between her lips and thighs. She felt a part of herself step up and stroll around the room, then turn and look back at her now in this halted moment: on her knees, body stinking, sweat sheening her skin; one man's baby in a cardboard box, one man's money on her table, one man's toys in her closet. All these things left behind, and here she was killing herself, trying to scrub away as many hours of the day as she could so she wouldn't have to face the fact that she was alone. "Oh God," she cried aloud. "Why does it have to matter?" She sat on her legs, cursing herself for crying, wondering why she felt so worthless just because nobody was there. Why did she have to feel that way ? Why couldn't she make a change?

Dandy started crying in repeated nasal sobs, "Na na na na na." When his hands curled onto the top of the cardboard box and he pulled himself up so his glasses were looking out over the top edge into the room, Jolene said aloud, "I just can't take it right now. I can't take anybody asking me for any more pieces of myself."

She threw the facecloth at the table but it fell short and splatted on the floor. Dandy kept crying and Jolene, crawling on her hands and knees toward the threshold, paused in her flight and twisted her head to yell back at him, "Nanananana yourself." He continued so she yelled it again. He started in louder and she raised her voice to match. He began a ululating cry and Jolene screamed "Aaahh! Aaahh! Aaaaaaahhhhhhh . . ." She held the scream until her lungs were sore and empty and she felt her face rush with blood. She was faint from the exertion.

She crawled into the bedroom, taking the pint bottle with her. She shut the door and flicked on the transistor radio to hear Linda Ronstadt, her favorite, singing "Love Is a Heartache." Don't it figure. "That's just a little bit too goddamn much," she told the room. She held the bottle in her hands for some minutes, singing along with the radio and looking at the label as if the words to the song were printed there. The song finished up and the commercials came on. Jolene screwed off the cap and flung it across the room.

The buzz in her head was loud and thick as she staggered to the kitchen, determined to do something about Dandy's crying. She lifted him from the box and almost fell over before she could get him to the floor. When she tried to back onto a chair so she could think for a minute, she missed and slammed down so heavily she bit her tongue. She figured she was in no condition to change his diaper. Once Artie had suggested she dunk Dandy in the toilet to clean him. At the time, she'd been horrified by the suggestion. Now the idea seemed pretty sensible. Even that, though . . . she'd probably drop him in. She saw Dandy spinning with the turds, his head and one arm reaching out as he was sucked down by the whirlpool. "No," she yelled, and leaned forward to grab him.

The kitchen came back to her, wavering, lining up, wavering again, like a film someone was trying to focus, and she realized she had actually been asleep. It had all been a dream. He wasn't in the toilet, he was on this floor. Maybe this was a dream too, this whole life of hers. She smiled and looked around for Artie; she actually called his name before she recalled that he was gone. He'd left her. No. She'd left him. "I kicked him out." She pouted at Dandy, who had pressed his hands against the stove and was trying to stand. She got real worried then; she didn't want to see him on his feet. Why did babies ever have to grow up and become like real people?

"I kicked him out because he hit you," she told Dandy. She dragged him awkwardly toward her, pulling him by one arm so he slid across the floor on his back. "Don't that mean nothing?"

Jolene shuffled over to the box on her butt and pulled out Dandy's bottle. She poured whiskey in with the Pepsi, more than she had intended. Some of it slopped onto her hand and she licked it off. The top of Dandy's bottle went on easily, and she thought of how things always went together much easier than they came apart. "I thought of that myself," she told Dandy. It made her feel mystical, full of wisdom. She stared at him, but Dandy was flat on his back, looking at the ceiling, not at her. "At least you could appreciate me. I could've dumped you in a bucket." She slid him up into her lap.

He took the nipple end readily, but spit it out and wailed when the liquid hit his tongue.

"Don't do this to me," Jolene yelled. With one hand pressing on his chest to hold him flat, she could feel his small ribs and the beat of his heart. Briefly she considered leaning forward and putting all her weight onto him until he cracked like a chicken. "Jolene," she told herself, stunned by her own thoughts. She tried to pray, hoping that would help her, make her a better person. "God get me out of this mess," she said. She wasn't sure that He was listening.

Dandy began crying so loud it didn't even help when she put her hands to her ears. "Who wound you up?" She bent close to his face. "Who wound you up?" The idea rooted, and she flipped him over onto his stomach. She searched under his T-shirt for the wind-up key. Maybe it was somewhere else. Maybe it was disguised. His belly button? His penis? She shook her head. "Jolene, now get ahold of yourself," she said. Of course there wasn't any real wind-up key. She was getting crazy on herself here. "Get ahold now, gal," she said. "Whoa, gal." She realized that she was talking like Artie. "Goddamn you!" she exclaimed. Then she figured, while she was at it, she might as well goddamn the other man too, that man whose name she didn't know. Now that she thought about it, she didn't even know Artie's last name.

The hell with it. It didn't matter. They were just seconds in her life. "Oh goddamn you, Dandy, please shut up."

She knew immediately what would work. Gripping the table edge to steady herself, she flopped one hand along the surface until she felt the sugar packets. She dragged several toward her. They tumbled to the floor before she could close her fingers on them.

Dandy was crouching, ready to attempt standing without support. Jolene grabbed his shirt. "Don't you go walking away on me too," she told him. She yanked so hard he fell into her lap. It surprised him into silence.

She ripped the top off a sugar packet and poured half of it onto Dandy's tongue. Then she quickly milked some of the whiskey mixture into his mouth. He shook his head but kept on mashing his tongue on the roof of his mouth to swallow the sugar. Jolene had to use three packets, but she was able to get a good deal of the bottle into him.

After he'd passed out and she'd put him back in his box, she sat by him for a while, feeling the tension of being alone grip her once again. She felt all twisted around and put together wrong. It was like someone had taken all the thoughts in her mind and rearranged them into some random order. Nothing made any sense to her. She looked at Dandy, his glasses pushed up onto his brow, his tongue rolling out of his mouth. He looked so small and cold. She shook him, but he didn't come awake, and she listened to his low breaths and the straining sound of someone crossing the floor above her ceiling. She couldn't remember why it had been so important for him to go to sleep.

# CHAPTER
# —11—

"What are you doing to me?" were the first words he said after the accident.

A doctor and two nurses, all younger than Artie, took quick half steps backward from the raised cot he found himself on. He was worried. When the Volkswagen had hit it had thrown him into the windshield with enough force to really crack the glass. The blood started coming and it was lights out for Artie. Every time he came around he saw the blood and passed out again. Then he heard them using that word—coma—and he figured he'd better open his eyes and find out what was what here.

Now the front of his head was numb, but he could feel the tug as they took up the stitches. Watching the needle and thread out of the tops of his eyes, he thought he was just some sort of doll being fixed, not a human being.

"What's your name?" the doctor asked. "Do you know who you are?"

"Do I know who I am?" Artie looked slowly at the three confused faces. How could they know? He never carried identification. Never needed it. And why give away information if you didn't have to? He tried to make his face all red and sweaty, so it'd look like he was concentrating. It wasn't too hard to do. All he had to do was think of Gristel. He stared at the fluorescent tubes on the pale green ceiling. "Who am I?" he said. "Ahh, Jesus, I can't remember. I don't know who I'm supposed to be." The doctor cleared his throat and then the three of them were all over him again.

He could tell they didn't believe him. But what did he care?

They couldn't do nothing about it. They couldn't just toss him out in the snow. Besides, they'd already told him they kept the victims with head injuries in the hospital for a while, for observation. He wasn't keen on that, people observing him. They'd see right away how normal he was. Maybe he could pretend somehow his head wasn't working right. He was sure that'd be pretty hard to do, but there was no sense quitting before he got started. Who knows, if things worked out he might end up with his own little room here while they tried to figure out who he was.

When they finished the stitches, Artie told them his legs were shaky so they sat him in a wheelchair and rolled him to the front.

"He can't remember who he is," the nurse pushing him told the older, redhaired woman at the desk.

"You're the so-called amnesia case?" the older nurse said to Artie. The counter was so high he could barely make her out. She had a girlish face regretfully giving in to age. She exchanged some sort of look with the nurse behind Artie, who was holding on to the handles of the wheelchair. "What's your name, really?" the nurse at the desk asked.

"You tell me, sweetheart, and I swear I'll love you forever," Artie said.

"John Doe, then." She bent her head as if she were writing on something.

"Whoa. Hold it now. Just cool your jets. Don't write nothing official now," Artie said, tapping his hand on the counter. The nurse looked over at him, her neck stretched and her face jutting forward. "Isn't that a deer?" he asked her.

"Excuse me?"

"Doe, a deer, a female deer; ray, a drop of golden suuuuuuun; me, a name I call myself; faaaaar . . ." He was ready to do the whole song but she reached across and tapped his lips once with her Bic pen. Control, Artie told himself. "I don't want to be named after no animal."

"Well, then, you pick one for yourself," she said, shaking her head.

"Any name?"

"That's right. Little Bo Peep if you'd like."

"Aw, give me a break," Artie said. She looked disgusted with him—they all looked disgusted with him in here. Goddamn public servants, he thought. When he got out he'd get ahold of somebody about that. Now he closed his eyes and rubbed his neck.

"Maybe he's a member of royalty," the nurse in front of him said.

"Maybe he's a president," the nurse at his back replied. They laughed.

"Why not?" Artie said. "I could be. I could be someone very important."

The nurse at the counter rolled her eyes. "Okay, we'll call you George Washington," she said.

"Uh-unh," he told her. "Anything but George."

"Does Abe Lincoln suit you better?" the nurse behind him said. They both laughed again.

"Too Jewish," Artie said. They shook their heads at each other. They were having a good time, he thought, acting like he wasn't even there. "What's the matter, two names and you got no more left in your brains?"

The nurse in front of him squinted angrily. Slowly her eyes opened as her smile grew. "You could be Richard Nixon."

"You can't do that," the nurse behind him said. She laughed some more.

"Why not?" Artie said. "He was a president?" He stroked his chin and nodded to himself. "Yeah. Richard. Rich. Yeah, I don't mind being Mr. Rich at all. You see me?"

"Too clearly," the redheaded nurse said and they both tittered. Artie didn't quite get that one, but he laughed anyways. No sense letting them know they were getting ahead of him.

The nurse at the counter wrote the name in so heavily that he could hear the pen scratch.

He wasn't sure how long he could pull it off, but he figured he might as well go for it. Things were pretty good. Free meals, TV, and if he didn't have the run of the place, at least it was comfortable. There was one other guy in his room—some old geezer who fell off his porch and had both legs in casts and wore a neck brace during the day, though he took it off at night when he slept. Artie heard that whole story the first five minutes he was in the room. The guy started right in moaning and complaining about being in pain and having no family to visit. Artie finally laid it out rational-like for the guy. "My stitches itch like a bitch," he said. "You don't think that's pain?" He touched the crooked line on his forehead. "And my whole family died in a fire when I was three years old. My old man had a wooden leg and he fell asleep one night with a lit cigarette. His leg caught on fire and burned up everything. I spent the rest of my life living in alleys and stuff, never having food or clothing or anything. Everything against me. Never getting one break. But you don't hear me complaining. This is a vacation, pal."

"If you have amnesia," the guy said, "how can you remember your family?"

"Fuck you," Artie told him. "And if you say one word to anybody, I'll choke you to death when you're asleep."

The guy never said another word after that and Artie figured, the hell with him if he didn't want to be friendly. Artie had the TV control anyways, so what did he need conversation for?

As the night went on he felt more cramped, trapped almost. It wasn't like he thought it would be. Sure, he had his meals and a bed and a TV. But it was just him. If Jolene was there it'd be perfect. He wondered, though, if she'd even open her door to him again. What'd he have to hit Dandy for? Why did Dandy have to be such a pain? Then he realized it wasn't Dandy, it was that goddamn Gristel, who ripped Artie off. That guy was the cause of all this. Artie tried to stay mad about that, but he was lonely for Jolene and he had trouble keeping his mind on anything else. He felt nervous, like he was missing something inside his skin. He didn't want to face that feeling, didn't want to think he couldn't enjoy a cozy setup like this, just because she wasn't there. Maybe he should grab himself a nurse. In his mind he went over them all, the ones he'd seen. Some of them were pretty, but he couldn't really picture himself sharing a bourbon with them or taking them dancing at Charley's. The more he thought, the more he came back to Jolene.

Each time he settled down to sleep he was tossed up again, shaken awake. He saw shadows diving through the darkness. Then too, this guy in the other bed. Who was he really? He could be some maniac who went around killing people at night, and Jolene wasn't there to look out for Artie.

Finally he just put the light on. There was nothing to do, though, and he sat for a while listening to the generators hum. In the drawer of the bedside table he found a piece of stationery and worked on it with his fingers, ripping and tearing in a slow, deliberate way, until he had a paper doll that looked like Jolene. Using a pencil, he poked a hole in the doll's forehead. He ripped a thread from the lower edge of his Johnny and tied it through the hole. "Jolene," he whispered, "Jolene." He spun the doll in a circle, feeling good that he could control its movements. But it was just a doll. Still, he hoped that somehow she could hear him and know he was thinking about her.

A nurse came in, making her rounds, and made him put out the light. He tried to talk to her, to get her to stay, but she had her rounds, there was no time. He lay in the dark, his arm extended, twirling the Jolene doll so it danced on his head. He felt like his skin had opened out and covered all the walls, so that his whole person was just this big empty space. He knew. He had to get out of there.

# CHAPTER
# —12—

She sat cross-legged on the mattress and held the fifth above her head. Golden bars of light streaked through the last inch of whiskey, making lines that curved with the glass. She couldn't remember if this was the day she'd bought the bottle or the day after she'd purchased it. Had she been drinking from this bottle for two days? Or one? She tried to think, but everything in her head felt fragmented.

With an apelike sideward sweep of her hand she dragged the transistor radio across the floor toward her. The small black box tumbled onto the bed, and she pinned it with her fingers so it wouldn't move on her. She clicked it on, spun the volume up, but there was no sound at all, not even static.

The damned batteries, she thought. They don't last any longer than the men in your life. She made to toss the radio onto the foot of the mattress, but when it left her hand it leveled off and flew past the bed. It hit the floor with a sharp, cracking sound and popped open. She half expected to see some small creature with antennae crawl forth. One battery rolled out, making a *chunka-chunka* sound as it crossed the floor and bumped to a halt against the far wall.

Dandy lay in his box, his tongue pushed out onto his bottom lip. His glasses were off and he was curled in one corner, taking in shallow, mucus-rattling breaths.

She set the bottle in front of the stove and leaned over the chair into the box. At first he was elusive, farther away than she'd thought. But when she did get her hands on him her angle was wrong, or her arms were too weak. Something. She couldn't lift him. She wanted to feel someone pressing on her, feel a human weight, but she couldn't get him out of his box. The hell with it, she thought. The first headache hit her then, a hammering pain that began at her wisdom teeth and slammed straight through the top of her skull. She closed her eyes and held her mouth open until the throbbing subsided to a beeping ache, like there was pressure in there she couldn't release. She gulped from the bottle to kill it, to get some sort of absence of mind.

She woke up in the bed. In her mind were traces of a movie she'd once seen about demons and witchcraft. There'd been a certain shape painted on the floor in somebody's house. If you stood inside the lines, it was a door to another dimension. She felt something like that about her bed. Only being on it would keep her where she was, stop her from going to another world.

She tried to imagine her room as an ocean filled with fish-shaped demons. Distorted heads and toothy mouths. When she looked around she expected to see them snapping out of the waves, trying to get her, and she made biting motions with her own mouth, as if fighting back. But the action made her remember the time in high school when she had suddenly found herself behind the poolroom, kneeling on the bricks and trash in the alley, the cement wall at her back, some boy's cock in her mouth, other boys waiting in line, feeling pleased at having people around her, her pleasure collapsing to sorrow when they all ran off at the end so nobody would see them with her.

She had trudged home then, watching the sunset spill toward her at every intersection like a warning that nothing would ever work, things would never get better. It was so incomprehensible, what she'd done, that she couldn't even feel ashamed. She had told herself things *would* get better. They would. Someday. When she grew up.

She looked at the dusty floorboards, bright in the light from the overhead. They were old and worn to a smooth, frayed finish, seamed with cracks that could not be fixed.

• • •

At some point she'd propped the cross with the dog's head on the window ledge. She was on the mattress, trying to decide what to do. Maybe she'd pretend she was in a movie. It took her some time to think, and she slugged from the bottle while she was waiting for the ideas to come. It was harder than she'd expected. She couldn't come up with a whole story, beginning, middle, and end, but she figured something about devils and rituals and sacrifices, moving back and forth through time. It'd be a comedy. She could use a laugh. But it'd be sad, too. She'd be two people, one good and one bad, trying to get together with herself. But she was all mixed up.

She closed her eyes and traveled to the dark dimension. She opened them and stared at her leader on the cross. The dog's head was so goofy it wasn't even funny. She had to be serious in this part because she was his slave in her soul, and she knew he was supposed to mate with her. She grabbed the whiskey bottle, tightened the cap, and laced her hands around the base. The glass was cool and firm. She'd done this once before. In the eighth grade. She'd sat on the infield of a baseball diamond, moving a Coke bottle in and out of her vagina, asking the boys sitting on the bench beyond the foul line, Who's next? How about you? They all had excuses. One of them said, "I have clean underwear on." At the time, she laughed with them. Now, that didn't seem so funny anymore.

She thought about that, how something could seem funny at one time in your life and not funny at all in another. What changed? she wondered, but she couldn't figure it out.

She thought of all the boys—in the playground, on the baseball field, behind the poolroom, at the gas stations. They were men now, going through their lives, moving God knew where around the world. Carrying stories with them. They'd probably tell everyone they met about the crazy girl and how they laughed at her. She imagined a network of moving people, pulsing around the world like blood moving through veins. She saw it all clearly in her mind, the round globe, veins circling it, the dark liquid passing through the veins. It was like she was watching it from a satellite in space. And then, for no reason she could control, for the second or third time in the last few days, she seemed to be looking at herself from outside her body. She saw herself stretched on a thin battered mattress in the middle of a dirty floor, a bottle clutched between her hands and aimed like a missile at her vagina; a black cross on the window topped by a stuffed dog's head. She was sick of it, sick of looking at herself this way. She didn't want to see what she was like anymore. A seizure of self-hatred shook her, and she wanted to ram the bottle inside herself so hard it would explode. But it passed like a current and she let go, let the bottle fall to the mattress. She stared at the loose weave of lines on her palms. The cross caught her eye and she looked at the dog's head. "This ain't funny, Artie." She wondered if she was possessed.

She knew what she should do. Get a job. That was the answer. Find someplace to spend her time. Someplace where she was wanted day after day. Where if she didn't show up they'd call—once she got a phone—and ask her how she was feeling, when she'd be back. Tell her they missed her and to hurry up and get back because they needed her. She'd never worked, though, except for the job at Burger King during high school, and she wasn't certain how to go about applying for a real job. Or even what she should be. The only thing she was certain of, she had to get dressed up.

She only had two dresses. One was a yellow summer outfit with a flingy bottom, so the choice was made for her. It would've been better to have a different choice, but it was either the yellow dress or the green one, which had a mandarin collar and puffy sleeves. Yellow daffodils were printed across it in rows, like a chorus of singing mouths. She looked at the mouths as she pulled it off the hanger. She wished she had something to sing about.

It took a while to pull the dress over her head. She thought it was because the headache made her stagger. She couldn't still be drunk. That was ridiculous. But it felt like her arms were swollen and too big to make it through the sleeves. That was ridiculous too. She was finally able to pull it down to a point even with her knees, and she fell back against the wall to catch her breath. A jarring pain pumped into her skull and she clenched her fists and doubled over, grimacing. If she could only poke a hole through her head, let that pressure out, she'd be okay. The pain kept at her like a scream. When it lowered its voice she lifted the bottle and tipped the last of the whiskey down her throat.

The only boots she had were her knee-high white plastic ones. They weren't exactly what she'd pick herself. Henry had bought them for her; he used to like to dress her up like a go-go dancer before they had sex.It was either the boots or sneakers, though, and she knew she had to get as dressed up as she could. It wasn't like going down to Welfare.

She wrestled with one boot, finally getting it turned around and pointing in the proper direction on her foot. When she tried to force her foot past the opening all the way to the bottom, she found herself falling into the closet. She banged against the back wall and slid heavily to the floor. Only then, inside the darkness, was she able to free her foot into the loose rub of the lining.

She pulled the other boot to her with her foot. Her toes were dirty and she realized she'd forgotten to put her tights on. The hell with it. No way could she take that boot off this minute. It was too much to ask. She needed a rest. Maybe she should put her makeup on first, before starting all over again with the clothes.

As she walked to the bathroom her left side bounced against the bedroom wall. The bouncing seemed to go along with the limp caused by the boot on her right foot, the two of them working together to keep her moving. The limp threw her forward so she tottered, but the wall bounced her back to a point of stability. It was a good thing the boot was on her right foot, she thought. Because if it was on her left she'd just careen into the middle of the room and God knows where she'd end up.

In the bathroom mirror her reflection was moving on her, making it hard for her to apply the blush. She thought of the image in the mirror as "that other Jolene," and once she even stroked a swath of blush onto the surface of the mirror. She knew it was crazy, of course it wouldn't work, but still, maybe that other Jolene, when she came back into the mirror, might pass through the blush spot and pick some up.

She was tipping backward. She dropped the brush and gripped the rim of the sink to stop herself from falling into the bathtub. The mirror slid down from view and she was looking at the ceiling but she held on and, pulling hard, steadily moved herself forward. She passed the balance point and her weight shifted. She tipped toward the mirror, afraid the force of her head would shatter the glass; that was all she needed, seven years of worse luck than this. She shut her eyes. There was a solid thud as her head bumped, but no sound of anything breaking.

For a second it was pleasant with her eyes shut, the world gone. But soon her head began to whirl. A galaxy was born inside her, all flashing lights and drifting gases, unshaped forms of matter, small bright explosions. It was too much to keep inside. She was afraid that if she went on with her eyes shut it'd spill out of her and overwhelm the kitchen, her apartment, maybe even the whole country.

She opened her eyes and blew out a long, slow breath. She hadn't known she'd been holding her breath, but the release of it made her feel tired, unprepared for the task of putting herself together for the world.

At least with her head against the medicine cabinet she felt stable. Maybe it'd be better for her to start with the eyeliner anyways. She didn't know if she was even capable of bending down to pick up the blush brush and make it back to a standing position.

She patted the back of the sink with one hand until she found the eyeliner pencil. She fumbled the top off, heard it clink on the floor. Pressing her forearms to the mirror to steady herself, she brought the thick black point to her skin.

It was all right, she told herself, the girls downtown were wearing eye makeup heavier this year. Still, when she looked in the mirror, she thought of football players, those wide smudges under their eyes like tire tracks. "It'll have to do." She dropped the eyeliner in the sink and flopped and bounced her way into the kitchen without falling. At the table she pushed over the chair she'd been intending to sit in. She fell on top of it. Holding her hands on opposite legs, she pushed herself back onto her feet. She held her arms out for balance and looked at Dandy's box. No sound came from there and she thought he was still, thank God, asleep.

"Mama's going to find a job just like a real mama," she said. She couldn't see him. The interior of the box was dark. She wondered if she was blacking out. She looked toward the window and couldn't see the building next door either. Was she going blind? She lurched to the window and fell against the cold glass, pressing her hands and face tight to it as she hit. Everything spun wildly and she couldn't control the motion. She whirled with it, and when the spinning slowed, and everything came together, she saw a series of waxy yellow squares. She stared at them for a long time. Only slowly did she come to understand that they were windows in the building across the way.

"Of course," she said, speaking as if correcting Dandy. "It's nighttime." She gathered the material of her dress front in her hands, rubbed it between her fingers, and told herself, "I did all this for nothing."

Her legs wavered backward and her knees buckled forward. She found herself kneeling, her chin to the bottom windowsill, the damp cold spreading from her nose across her face. She turned and, pushing the chair from the front of Dandy's box, stretched out on the floor. She decided she'd think about her life. That's what she'd do. While she was all dressed up and everything, in the right attitude and all, she might as well think hard about it. She looked at the floor around her face, as flat and empty as a desert. She was going to think about her life if it was the last thing she'd ever do.

A roach scampering across her cheek woke her to the pain and ache of alcohol and a night spent on a draft-swept floor. She was capable of squinting down the pain and washing her face off, which made her feel less greasy, if no more comfortable. Her flesh in the mirror looked loose and pulpy, and no amount of makeup could hide that fact. But she was going to go out anyways and make somebody hire her. There had to be something she could do. She cleaned off her dress as best she could, pulled it tight at the hem in an attempt to straighten out the wrinkles, put on her tights, and washed her boots off with a wad of damp toilet paper.

As she was about to leave, Dandy woke up crying. She knew it had to be his diapers or food. There was nothing she could do about either. Not then. From the doorway she saw his eyes peek over the box; they moved around like a clock face in a cartoon after all the insides had been sprung.

She was afraid he'd get out, and the irrational image of him walking down the sidewalk carrying a small suitcase played in her mind. She remembered something about the Chinese, binding the feet of their women so they wouldn't run away. Taking the piece of rope from the cross in the closet, she noosed Dandy's feet together. He grabbed at her hair and she had to uncurl his fingers to get away. She took some crackers from the cupboard, put one in his mouth, and dropped the rest in the box around him.

She hit the street without a plan. The sun was a formless yellow spill in the ash-white sky, and somehow that light didn't give her much sense of hope. Most of the snow had melted, with only humps gathered on the corners, spread with a speckled coating of black dirt. She'd try everything, she told herself. Every business she came to. One right after the other until something clicked. If it took her two months of walking this city, she'd find a job. Somebody out there must be willing to pay her for something.

A variety store's small red and white sign shone across the street. Checking around first, to make sure no one was watching, she pulled up the crotch of her black tights, then headed for the door.

# CHAPTER —13—

He couldn't hardly move without someone jumping all over him. "This is a hospital, not a country club," one nurse said to him the third time she found him wandering the halls.

"I just want to talk to somebody," he said.

"Talk to your roommate." She led him to his room.

"See you around," Artie said at the door.

"If we find you in the hall one more time," she told him, holding her finger in his face, "we'll put you in restraints."

That was it for him. He was through with this joint. He hung out in bed the rest of that day, trying to come up with some plan. Mostly he just rolled around on the mattress, flipping stations like he was dealing cards, missing Jolene. At ten minutes to eight the warning came over the intercom that visiting hours were almost over.

"That's something, a last call for visitors," Artie said, but the guy beside him was sound asleep. On the table between the two beds, the neck brace was a dull tan curve.

He tried it on. It didn't feel too bad. Maybe it'd be good for suing somebody. He didn't know who, exactly, but if he had one of these he could sue someone. Somebody had to owe him money for something. Maybe he could get hit by a bus, show up in court—Your honor, my life is ruined. He felt close to an idea when the rapid slap of feet in the hallway beat his mind clear. He couldn't turn fast enough to see what was up. "I got no periphery," he said. "All I can see is what's before me. You know?"

He shifted around to the old guy, who was still zonked out. Out the window the snow-covered lawn was a soft blue-white from the light of the moon. White lights on top of silver poles sprayed bright funnels around the parking lot. There were a number of people going to their cars. This was it, he thought, and he hurried to get dressed. He slipped into the corridor behind a family of six and slid with them right past the nurse's station, through the waiting room, and out the door. When he told an elderly couple about the problem with his car, how it wouldn't start, they gave him a ride to the nearest Howard Johnson's.

"Neck problems?" the man asked, moving his lips like he was chewing on something.

"Yeah," Artie said. "I got in an accident."

The man touched the back of his neck. "I still have some shrapnel from the war."

"Yeah, yeah, me too," Artie told him as they pulled up to the front door. Artie thanked them for the ride, opened the door, and paused with one foot out. "Oh God, I left all my money in the car," he told them. They gave him a $5 bill and he wrote their names down so he could mail it back to them.

"We have a son too," the woman said, patting his hand on the back of the seat.

"I love my mother," he told the lady, and they decided to give him another $5.

It took him a while to hitch back into town. He thumbed a ride halfway with a truck driver, got a few more miles from some high school kids who took him by a liquor store so he could buy them rum; then another trucker gave him a ride to a 24-hour pancake house only thirty minutes outside the city. By the time Artie got there the place was full of drunken kids, just out of high school, who'd come there when the bars closed. Artie bought a coffee and settled in for the night. He needed a plan. He needed to set up something. If he went straight to Jolene's and didn't get in, that'd be that. He didn't know what the hell she wanted from him, and that made it harder for him to figure out what to do. "What do broads want these days?" he asked the waitress when she refilled his cup, but she acted like he was diseased just for asking her a question. Kids, he thought. They should respect adults.

He gulped from his cup, liking the way the coffee almost burned his throat. Things needed some fixing here, he thought. But where could he go to figure it out? No way could he go back to Denny's; Smitty might be there looking for him, and Artie wasn't ready for that kind of trouble. He needed time and a place. Maybe he should've stayed at HoJo's. Started off fresh in the morning. Maybe he could've sleazed his way in with those old people, if he'd played his cards differently. At a table across the restaurant a pimple-faced boy vomited all over a stack of pancakes. "Jesus Christ, I gotta take you home to your mother," his friend said, pulling the sick boy up by the sleeve.

Artie looked into his coffee cup, matching the curve of the rim with his lips. That was it. The place he needed. The one place he'd be let in, no questions asked. He settled back in the booth, feet up, and slept until daylight.

He looked around the tight front room like a mover appraising the place. Wedged into a rocker in the far corner was the slab who was his mother's latest boyfriend. But did the guy get up to shake Artie's hand? No. Neither did his mother. She just sat there on the matching scarlet couch, leaning on the arm closest to the chair.

Artie walked the length of the couch and turned his back to them. He stared at the painting on the wall, pretending to study it while he tried to get a handle on the situation. He felt out of place, and he hated the feeling. Who was this guy? Why hadn't Artie's mother told him? He didn't seem like her usual boyfriends. He seemed permanent. And where did all this furniture come from? It was the same apartment, but it didn't feel like the place he'd grown up in.

"This new?" he asked, nodding at the painting.

"Artie, ain't you got eyes and a mind to remember with? It's all new. The chair, the couch, the rug . . . Joey brung them from his place when his mother finally kicked off."

"Hey, a little respect here," Joey said.

Artie heard his mother say, "Yeah, yeah, I'm sorry." He glanced at the gold shag rug beneath his feet. It was too large for the room and it crept up the base of the walls all around. He lifted one shoe, moving it as if he expected the thick fibers of the rug to cling to his sole like glue. There was no resistance and he looked back at the painting.

It was four feet long and a foot and a half high. It seemed to be a cross between an oil painting and a 3-D background for a fish tank. The scene was the interior of a palace, with pools of black fabric surrounding a central fountain. The fountain was double-tiered, with a harp-playing cherub standing atop it. Looping plastic lines representing water curved from the cherub's mouth down to the first tier, then to the base, which opened in petals. Four columns were inset around the fountain, and the fountain itself pushed out in relief, as did the palm trees that ran from top to bottom at each edge of the painting. The trunks of the trees were formed from rough clear plastic, segmented to look like bark. Scattered throughout were vases, tables, and gourds in bright oranges, greens, and purples. A cord hung from the middle of the bottom frame, the plug dangling loose in front of a light socket.

"Put it on," his mother said; then she spoke to Joey. "It's okay, he won't break it."

Artie sunk the plug into its socket. The palm trees burned golden. Golden drops, like dotted lines, spilled from the cherub's mouth and filled both tiers of the fountain. At the bottom, blue lights blinked in what was intended to be the illusion of moving water, waves. The drops never stopped falling.

"Ain't that something?" his mother said.

"Too much class for this shithole," Joey said.

"All right already, I heard it before, okay? Only about a million times. I'm sorry it ain't as nice as your mother's place, but you're the one didn't want to stay there," she said.

"What're you, an idiot? How many times I got to tell you? Anyone knows I can't have you sleeping in my mother's bed. Jesus Christ." The palm tree on the right started blinking. Behind Artie, Joey said, "Goddamn this place."

Artie turned and watched the man heft himself to his feet

with difficulty. He wallowed through the muddy light of the room and pushed Artie aside.

"Easy, Buster," Artie told him, but Joey ignored him. Artie looked at the back of the man's head. The hair was thin and greasy, and his skull was five times the size of Artie's fist.

Joey tapped his balloon fingers onto the palm tree three times, blessed himself, then hit it three times again. The light stayed on. "There's something fucked up in the walls of this joint. Negative currents."

"Maybe it's a loose bulb," Artie said.

"Where'd you dig him up?" Joey said to Artie's mother.

"I'm her kid. Her and Frankie the Weasel's," Artie said to the side of Joey's head.

"That's what you think," Joey said without looking at him, and he huffed his way across the room to the chair.

"What's this shit?" Artie asked. His mother looked away.

Joey rocked back and looked at Artie's mother. "Know who he reminds me of? With that thing on his neck. Now think of it, and tell me if I ain't right. Tattoo?" Joey rolled up on one hip and pulled a gray handkerchief from his back pocket. The sweat on his face was so thick it looked splashed on. He smeared the beads to a thin sheet with the handkerchief before blowing his nose.

"Ma, you going to let him talk to me like that?" Artie felt like popping the guy. But it was her place. Her responsibility. The guy was big, too.

"What am I supposed to do, fight your battles?" Everything about her looked swollen: the full, wavy black hair, so thick you couldn't see her scalp; her square-boned face, with its puffy flesh; the thick lips that lay on her face like cocktail frankfurters; and her enormous breasts, which rolled down to rest on the top curve of her stomach. He was glad she was sitting down. He knew what he looked like, standing beside her. All his life he'd been embarrassed to be seen with her. He was the only person he knew who was still shorter than his mother.

"It's your place, you set the rules," he said. Joey flipped him the finger, but Artie pretended not to see it. Is this home or what?

"Artie, you're what? Thirty-six, thirty-seven? For Chrissakes, at that age you ain't supposed to be a son anymore, but a grown-up responsible man who's related to your mother by birth."

That confused him. He knew it was his turn to say something, but what? He looked at the rug, then back up at her. "You ain't my mother no more?"

"What'd I just tell you? You never did listen to nobody. No, I ain't your mother. Not in that sense."

"What sense are you talking about?"

"What sense am I—do I have to spell everything out for you? I swear to Jesus, Mary, and Joseph you're thicker than your old man. Look, at this point you're supposed to be a comfort to me. But look at you, Artie. I know you ain't never going to amount to something, but you got to stop being a zero all your life."

"Here we go again, for Chrissakes." He took two steps backward and looked up at the drop ceiling. "I'm looking over my options."

"Artie, you ain't got no options. You never had none, and you won't tomorrow neither." She lit a cigarette and threw the match into the open mouth of a frog ashtray on the coffee table. At her back the window was covered with a white gauze curtain. Two windows of the brick building across the way were visible through the thin fabric. Faces were peering across at them.

"I'm going to get a lot of money from this," Artie said. He put one hand to his neck in a choking gesture. "I'll be a millionaire. I'll buy you a new house, a car. . . ."

His mother puffed smoke rings toward the ceiling. She pointed at him with the two fingers holding the cigarette. "I'm not about to put you up anymore on promises of going to and someday. For Chrissakes, Artie, you ain't been out of the house more'n three–four years tops, and you're what? Thirty-eight? Thirty-five?"

"That ain't true. I been on my own a long time."

"Yeah, maybe a long time if you count from the first year you moved out. But it was a week here, a week there, and then Mama

I'm back. If you count up the days like arithmetic, it's only been a few years. Besides, the last couple times you was here there was money missing. Now I ain't accusing you, but I can't afford you no more."

"We got no room for you, kid," Joey said. "We got something going and you'd be in the way."

"Use your brain, Artie," his mother told him.

"Hey, did I say I wanted to move back in?" He was getting that shaky feeling again.

"You don't have to. Anyone looks at you can tell. Artie, there's dirt falling off your clothes," she said.

"You get it on my rug, and you're going to have to vacuum," Joey told him, rocking hard to emphasize his point.

Artie waved his hand before his face. "Look, I told you, I don't want to move back here."

"Well, you can't," his mother said.

"I just said I don't want to. Who the hell needs it? Have you yapping at me all the time. I don't need that shit."

"Watch your mouth around your mother." Joey stopped the rocker to make his point. Then he cranked backward to show he meant business.

"I never yapped at you," his mother said. She watched the ash fall from her cigarette to the rug.

"Like hell you didn't. That's all you did. You ruined my life, for Chrissakes, you yapped so much."

"Hey, I'm warning you, show some respect," Joey said, rocking furiously. His lips began to blubber.

"When did I yap?" She ground the ashes into the rug with the toe of her spike-heeled boot. "I may have given you the shit, but I never yapped at you."

"All the time you yapped at me. I never had a moment's peace, for Chrissakes. You yapped at me to get a job, give you money, find my own place, don't be like my father. You're yapping at me now and I ain't even moved back yet."

"You ain't moving back, kid or no kid."

"I don't want to move back."

"And I ain't yapping."

"What the hell you think you're doing?"

"I ain't yapping. I'm giving you the shit."

"What's the fucking difference?"

"Boy, I'm getting mad now," Joey said. He gripped both chair arms and rocked so hard he thumped against the floor.

"Cut it," his mother told Joey. She turned to Artie and put her hands straight out, palms down. Smoke curled from the cigarette in her mouth and formed a thin, hazy screen in front of her face. She crinkled her nose and shifted to a high-pitched nasal tone, the cigarette bobbing as she spoke. "Yapping is like this—*neh neh neh neh neh*. You yap about things that don't count much. Giving you the shit is more like this"—she stretched her face loose and spoke in a slow, deep manner—"*nuh nuh nuh nuh nuh*. Giving you the shit is something you should listen to. Like right now, I'm giving you the shit about wanting to move back in here. If I was complaining about the price of peas, I'd be yapping at you."

"Jesus Christ, Ma—words? How am I ever supposed to understand you if you use words on me like that?"

"Don't you ever take the name of your Savior in vain," Joey said. He pointed to a picture of Jesus on the wall above the knickknack shelf to the left of the TV. The picture was a 3-D color version of a open-armed Jesus standing on a mountain. When Artie moved his head, Jesus brought his hands together in prayer. I'm not having none of that, Artie thought.

He turned to Joey. "Don't tell me what to do. You ain't my father."

Joey pushed back in the rocker and glowered at Artie's mother. "It's a good thing you're over there," Joey told Artie, showing him a meaty fist, "or I'd cold-cock you."

"You and whose army?" Artie stepped to the foot of the chair, careful to stay just out of Joey's reach.

"It's a good thing you're on my good rug that I don't want to get blood on, or I'd knock your head up your ass." Joey pushed the rocker back as far as it went.

"It's a good thing you're in my mother's house that I don't want to mess up on her." Artie stepped backward and showed his fist.

"It's a good thing I already been to confession and can't afford no murders on my soul for Sunday."

"Well, it's a good thing—"

"Jesus! Enough good things here to choke a horse. Now both of you just knock it off." His mother stubbed her cigarette out in the frog's throat. Waving her hand at Artie, she said, "Get over in that corner. And you, Joey, put your goddamned feet on the floor before you break the chair legs. Now, the both of you keep your mouths shut. Okay? Let's all be friends and adult-like here, okay?"

Artie stood by the knickknack shelf. There was only one item there, a piece of stained wood on which a furry green frog sat. The frog's hands were folded across its stomach, its marble-like eyes gazing upward, its mouth twisted down in a frown. Beside the frog was an empty shot glass. On the front of the wood ran the legend, *If I Don't Get A Drink I Will Croak.* Artie knew it was a present his father had given his mother for their first anniversary. That was the year his father bought presents for both of them. The first year he began to disappear for months at a time. But he loaded them up with gifts. Artie got his stuffed dog then.

He remembered it all, the presents and the leaving. Even more, the coming back. Artie had felt it was somehow his fault, and he should do something to keep his father home. He could never figure out what, though, and in a couple of years his father was gone for good.

"You couldn't beg me to come home," he told his mother. He thought about the frog. Maybe he should get something nice like that for Jolene. Something they could share. Something that might mean something.

"Then what are you doing here?"

"I just want to talk to somebody, that's all."

She shifted nervously on the couch and looked fearfully at Joey. "I don't know, Artie. I ain't never been a talker." She pulled a cigarette from the pack beside the ashtray and tapped the butt on the table. "Are you in trouble?"

"Not that kind of trouble."

"What do you mean, 'that kind'?" Beside her, Joey made soft grumbling noises in his throat. She hushed him. "There's only one kind of trouble, Artie."

He ran his fingers over the frog and turned to face her. "I think I'm in love." The words made him feel like a jerky little kid. Joey laughed like Woody Woodpecker.

"Jesus Christ, you almost gave me a heart attack," his mother said. "Trouble. I thought it was something important. What, you want my permission or something?" Joey's laugh continued in a long, twittering stream.

Artie thought of taking the shot glass and shoving it down Joey's throat. "You find that funny? You love my mother, don't you?"

"What a question," Joey said. He laughed harder, wiping the tears from his eyes with the heel of one hand.

"Ssshh," Artie's mother said to Joey. "Now shut down your noise. C'mere, Artie." She patted the cushion with her left hand and Artie noticed her rings were gone. He'd never seen her without them. It felt like he'd lost something.

He dropped his hand from the shelf to the TV on the stand beside him. In the dust on the top he drew wavy parallel lines, horizontal and vertical, intersecting in the middle.

"I don't know." She picked the cigarette from the table and stabbed it into her mouth. "What am I supposed to do? What's the problem? If you're sure, just go to City Hall for the ceremony. She's not a colored, is she?"

"Ma," Artie said, shaking his head.

"How am I supposed to know? These days, people being liberal and all . . ." She snapped the match to flame and took a long, luxurious inhale. "What's the problem then?"

"She doesn't want to talk to me."

"So? How much you think I talked to Frankie?"

"No, I mean, she won't let me in her apartment."

"That can make things difficult," Joey said.

Artie's mother waved at Joey to get him to shut up. "C'mon now, this is a mother-son sort of thing, okay?" She looked at Artie and took a slow drag on her cigarette. "What'd you do?"

"It's a long story."

"My shows are on in a few minutes. I ain't got time for long stories."

"Well, I didn't want to tell it anyways."

"Good, because I don't want to hear it," Joey said.

"I wouldn't tell *you.*"

"I already said I wouldn't listen," Joey said. "I said I wouldn't listen before you said you wouldn't tell it."

"You did not," Artie told him.

"I did too."

"Did not."

"Did too."

"Will you just clap your trap?" Artie yelled. He slammed his hand on the TV. Dust clouds spurted up and he sneezed. "I feel like I'm talking to myself here, going in circles." He pulled the coffee table forward with his foot so he could get to the couch, where he flopped onto the far end, sliding so his shoulders were almost on the cushions.

From the apartment next door an opera blared and the three of them covered their ears and gave out involuntary cries of pain. The music softened to a background noise and they sat in silence. The only sound was the soft crackle of his mother's cigarette as she smoked it, followed by the wheeze of her exhales. The light in the room thickened.

"Do you really like her, or do you just want to get back in?" his mother asked.

"What difference does it make? Of course I want to get back in. You got to have some place to go, right? But I like her too." He scrutinized his hands, the lines, the way his fingers moved. It made him think of Dandy's hands. How they were so little but just like real human hands, with fingernails and fingerprints and lines and everything. He got to thinking about babies, how they were miniature people. He'd never looked at it that way before, and it gave him a sudden urge to go take a look at the kid.

"It makes all the difference," his mother said. "If you like her, bring her flowers. If you want to get back in, bring some cans of tunafish. That's my advice. Everybody likes tunafish."

Artie looked at his reflection on the TV screen. It was like another, smaller person was in there. He looked at the reflections of his mother and Joey, leaning close to each other. That made him feel lonely. He didn't know how to explain it, him and Jolene, to his mother. He felt screwed up by words. He thought of something as he watched his mother pat Joey's arm. "We got along good too, you know?" he said. "I mean, we could do anything. We even used to fart together."

"Fart?" She fumbled with a new cigarette from the pack. "Is that what you said?"

"Yeah," said Artie. "Do I mumble?"

She pushed away from him as far as the couch would allow.

"Beans beans the musical fruit," Joey sang in a loud flat voice. "The more you eat the more you—" He rolled up on one hip and let out a short pop.

"The two of you," Artie's mother said, shaking her head.

"It wasn't like that. It was classy," Artie said. "It was something between us, you know? Something we shared. Like, Here's a message for you darling. That sort of thing."

Artie watched his mother's reflection in the TV. She shook her head and opened her arms. "Dear Jesus in heaven, what are you doing to me?"

"Don't you understand? Don't you see?"

"Far be it for me to tell you what to do, Artie, but"—she spoke with her cigarette bobbing between her lips—"did you ever think of, maybe, kissing her?"

Artie rolled his head over to look at her. "Ma. Of course I kissed her. That ain't the point. You can kiss a million people. How many people can you fart with?"

"I never counted." She looked over at Joey, who had settled back and closed his eyes.

"Most women you can't fart with," Artie said.

"I'm not surprised." She watched Artie out the corner of her eye.

"Ma, come on now," he said. "Don't you see? It's like—it's like . . . it's like a show of trust, right? You can always find someone to kiss, but how many times do situations last long enough that you can fart at each other?"

"Artie, please now, you're making me sick."

He shook his hands, trying to work out an explanation. "All right, let me give you this, okay? A for instance. You got a nice romantic dinner, right? The kid's mess has been changed, the Sloppy Joes are done cooking, the lights are out, just a little light from the streetlight coming in the window to help with the mood. You crack open a beer and take turns swigging on it. Jolene says to me, Are you really happy here? Only, instead of answering, I give her a fart—that's what I think about it, I say. We both crack up, then she says, Here's a love kiss for you, and she farts. That kind of closeness. I mean, what could be more romantic?"

She shook her head at the floor.

"Ma, come on now, don't do this to me. This is serious. I done things with her I never done with anybody." He leaned toward her.

"Artie, please, spare me the details." She exhaled a warning column of smoke into his face.

He sat back. "Didn't you and Frankie ever fart together?"

"What I did and didn't do with Frankie the Weasel is none of your business," she said quickly. She looked beside her, but Joey's head was tipped onto one shoulder. He made a blubbering noise and his thick-lidded eyes opened halfway. He appeared disoriented. He hauled himself from the rocking chair and crossed into the kitchen. The bathroom door slammed shut.

His mother put her cigarette in the frog's mouth and shoved one hand into the tight front pocket of her dungarees. She pressed several crumpled bills into Artie's hands and motioned for him to hide them quickly. She watched the doorway while he shoved them into his pocket. "This is what happens," she said, nodding toward the kitchen, "if you wait too long. Your choices are limited."

"Why do it then? If you're not hot for him. Why not look around?" Artie suggested.

She looked over at him. "Look around where?" She picked up her cigarette and dragged on it. "Do you have any idea how quiet it gets in here?" She exhaled and chewed on her bottom lip. "You got to take what's available. If you get along all right, so much the better. Go back to your Darlene."

"Jolene."

"Darlene, Jolene, Suzy—I don't care. Don't make no difference. It's just somebody to be with. Go back, and buy her something to keep her happy." She blew a funnel of smoke into his face. "Do something right for a change."

He nodded. "I will."

She smiled, then ground the cigarette out in the ashtray. "But give yourself a shave first," she said. "You look like shit."

# CHAPTER —14—

It's all something to do with fingers, she thought five hours later, as she hobbled along the streets on the fringes of the downtown shopping district. The blisters on her heels and toes made it difficult for her to walk more than half a block at a time without halting to let the pain subside.

In this part of the city the businesses were less glamorous, less threatening. The storefronts were formed from rotted, sooty wood that gave way to the step; the owners all seemed to need shaves, and they kept cigars or cigarettes clenched in their mouths, letting the smoke escape between their teeth with their words. Their eyes rarely made it up to her face as she tried to talk to them.

The hell with it, she decided. It wasn't worth it anymore. Even if there had been openings, she didn't have the experience with the finger things: typing, shorthand, sewing, cash register keys, piece work. The only possibility she'd come across all day had been at Bickford's Cafeteria. The manager told her she could bus tables and run the dish machine. He showed her the back room, the clanking machine with the steam pouring out of it, the barrel of garbage a small cloud of flies flew around. She told him she'd go to hell before she'd clean up everybody else's garbage.

She was on the corner opposite the hot dog stand beneath Artie's old apartment. The window was blocked with a blanket, giving the impression of an impenetrable darkness. She wondered if he was staying there again. She wanted to go in. With a furtive motion she took a mouthful of whiskey from the bottle she'd just bought. Why'd he have to go and hit Dandy? She dropped the bottle back inside her coat pocket. Something rushed through her, some emotion she couldn't define. It left her feeling drained and cheated. She yelled at the window, "I don't owe you a goddamn thing."

She looked around—the main street at her back was busy with people, all of whom seemed to have slowed down to watch her. She ducked her head and hobbled away, down the patchy side road.

She felt worthless. All day she'd listened to men tell her why she wasn't even good enough for them to hire her for dumb jobs which might, maybe, let her take home $100 a week. And that was for forty hours of her time. She couldn't believe she wasn't even worth that. Who were they to tell her she had so little value? She was sick of it. She was sick of men. All her life they'd been taking from her anytime they wanted something, and now when she need a stupid lousy job she wasn't good enough. They wouldn't even give her a chance.

She stepped in a pothole and almost fell, but was able to flay her arms out fast enough to maintain her balance. To her right was a parking lot; past that, down the street, an X-rated bookstore with thick meshed bars covering the windows. Across the street was the bar Artie had taken her to at night when they were starting out. She stood in front of the bookstore and looked at the bar, remembering the drinks and the dancing in the orange glow of the EXIT sign. What had happened to them?

A car pulled to a halt beside her. The driver motioned to Jolene with his hand, calling her closer. She looked around, then stepped forward, figuring he wanted directions. She checked over the car—a large silver four-door sedan with red velour interior—and touched the vinyl roof with her hand. The man reminded her of the one who had given her the ride. They both had gray hair and wore suits.

"How much?" he said.

She looked at him, confused, and asked, "For what?"

"Oh, that's right, entrapment." He nodded to himself and faced the steering wheel. His hands gripped the tube and rubbed back and forth against it. She watched his face turn a dark red as he mumbled to his horn, "For a blow."

She couldn't believe it. "I'm looking for a job," she said. "That's why I'm here."

In her mind she went over the things she had done that day. She'd had to sit on metal folding chairs, plastic milk cases, and wooden benches to fill out application forms, using her free hand to support the papers. She'd had to leave most of the questions blank—jobs, references—and then put up with interviews with men who were either bored or amused by her. She recalled shaking heads, ashes flicked in her direction, men wiping their mouths on their sleeves and telling her, "No way, sweetheart," or "Can't do it, honey," as she begged them to let her work for them.

"Hey," a woman's voice called out. It was harsh and stony. Jolene looked over to her right to see a black woman at the end of the street. She wore a spotted rabbit-fur coat, tight black slacks, and red spike heels. She shook her fist at Jolene and yelled, "This ain't your territory." Jolene looked down at her own coat, the white boots.

"How does twenty dollars sound?" the man said, his voice shaky. He checked his rearview mirror. "Hurry up. I don't want trouble."

Jolene looked at him, but he avoided her gaze. She said, "Don't do this to me." She looked back at the woman, who was shaking her fist and moving closer. Jolene thought, Who's she to tell me anything?

"Thirty dollars?"

"I'll kick your ass," the woman yelled. Jolene stared down at the tar, which was white with salt and age.

"Forty dollars," the man said.

Jolene rubbed her forehead with one hand. She couldn't believe this was happening to her. She felt the last of the money she had, $12, in a loose crumpled ball in her coat pocket. The woman yelled again, louder, closer. She was getting on Jolene's nerves. She felt besieged, but without clear choices. Invisible forces pressed in around her from all sides. She felt squeezed, limited; but distanced, somehow, too.

"Look, forty is it, the limit. That's it. I can't go any higher." He looked in his rearview mirror again. "Forty-five. Please, we're running out of time."

The woman was running toward them now and Jolene had the urge to wait for her. She felt like slapping her across the face. But that wouldn't solve anything either, she thought, and she looked at the man. He was shaking, he was so scared. He shifted the column stick from Park to Drive but kept his foot on the brake. She told herself, Forty-five dollars, ten minutes. Who would know? She hurried to the passenger side door.

She sat and held her hand out for the money. The car jerked to a start, then moved slowly, and the man passed her four tens and one five. She folded the bills and slipped them inside her boot.

She watched the bar as they pulled away. A man with a thin, worn face stood in the doorway. She held her breath, thinking it was Artie. The car moved forward and she watched the man over her shoulder. It probably wasn't Artie. It didn't have to be Artie. He had a different coat on. It could've been anybody. The black woman, hands on her hips, strolled over to the man and moved her mouth like she was complaining. The man looked the woman up and down. It better not be Artie, Jolene thought. She shuffled around and relaxed into the plush seat and immediately felt depressed. But she also felt, oddly, like she had won something, though she didn't quite know what.

They halted at the stop sign at the end of the road. She looked up at the window with the blanket tacked on the inside of it. Someone held it aside from inside, but she couldn't see them. She was afraid she was going to cry, so she dipped her head to the man's lap.

"Hey, wait until we're out of traffic. Someone might see," he said.

"It don't matter," she said as she undid his zipper.

"It matters to me," he said. "I have—well, you know—I can't be seen doing this."

She didn't listen. She pulled his penis out of his underwear and started to work. She wished her teeth were razor blades. She'd close her jaws and slice him off cleanly. Bite them all off, she thought. Every one in the goddamn world. Then she wouldn't be where she was, doing what she was. Just remember, she told herself: You have to take care of Dandy. She worked on the man as fast as she could. She wondered if this was what she deserved, after all. This was only her second time, but it was already easy.

The man was moaning, taking corners fast, and she worked harder. How could this happen? she asked herself. It's all for Dandy, she repeated in her mind, over and over, and she fought with herself so she wouldn't hate him too.

# CHAPTER
# —15—

There'd been no answer to his knock, so he put the brown shopping bag down and worked the key to open the door. "Jolene? You here?" he called, sticking his head into the room. He stepped in quietly, dragging the bag by its top. It felt like he was stepping into a memory. Everything was familiar, but there was something missing.

"Jolene?" The hum of the word vanished so quickly he wondered if he had really said it. He shut the door with his foot and moved the bag across the floor with a series of sliding kicks, keeping his hands open at his sides, away from his body. He stopped beside the table. It was *him*. He was missing. It didn't feel like *he* was in here anymore. That unsettled him, and he called her name again.

A quick scrabbling sound made him jump. Then Artie saw it was Dandy, standing up in his box.

"Dadadadada-daaa," Dandy said. He smiled and chewed on the cardboard.

"Ssshhh," Artie warned him. "Jolene?" His muscles were tense, his nerves tingling, and he felt the same rush of fear and glee that he got when he broke into apartments, the same sense of temporary yet complete power over the emptiness around him. Only it was less intense now, because he knew Jolene, if she wasn't there, would be coming back and he'd have to answer to her for any destruction.

"Dada-dadada."

"Don't start causing me trouble," Artie said. "I ain't your dada. You got that?"

"Bub bub bub." Dandy's eyes spun around wildly.

"The name's Artie. Ar-tie. Ar-tie."

Dandy shook as if trying to dance. He snuffled air out of his nose, then tipped his face toward the ceiling and yelled, "Bub bub bub bub bub!"

Artie wondered if Jolene had a new boyfriend. Some guy named Bub. With his head still, his eyes scanned the room looking for signs: cigarettes, bottles, or underwear. With her luck she'd pick somebody with that name, he thought, but he didn't see hints of anybody new.

"Dadadadada-dada." Dandy sneezed and fell down inside the box.

"Can't win," Artie said. He listened to Dandy's tentative whimpers. "Not this again. Jolene! Jolene! Your kid's acting up." He checked the other room. The bed had been slept in and he knelt on it, sniffing for odors of other men. He couldn't be sure. He noticed the bathroom door was shut, and he moved to it cautiously and pushed it open with one hand. He craned his head around the doorframe to look, but there was no one in there. He snooped around for signs—a toothbrush, whiskers, dark hair clogging the bathtub drain. Nothing, only a blush brush on the floor.

Certain that she wasn't home, he relaxed, rolling his shoulders to loosen the tension. It took the edge off, but his bones were vibrating at a low frequency and he had to piss three times in the next ten minutes.

He peeled off the neck brace, set it on the table, and circled his head to stretch his neck muscles.

"Man, the things I do," he said, not knowing what he meant by it but saying it real loud. He pulled Dandy from the box. There was a piece of rope tied around the kid's feet, and that upset Artie. Kid or no kid, nobody had a right to do that. You can't tie someone down like that. Jolene, he thought to himself, Jolene Jolene Jolene. Dandy stopped sobbing and grabbed at Artie's face.

"Don't mess with my meal ticket," Artie said as Dandy pulled at his lips with small, warm fingers. Where he rested on Artie's arm, Dandy's bottom was damp, and Artie was afraid of what that meant.

He laid Dandy on the floor and took one of the kid's hands. He held it so the palm faced up and placed his own larger hand beside it. They *were* alike, and Artie thought, I'll be damned. He laughed, and that made Dandy laugh. The kid's laughing made Artie laugh some more. There ain't much to it, taking care of kids. He finished untying the rope and Dandy kicked his feet. Artie leaned away, then bent over to undo the diaper. Not much to it at all, he thought. Then he saw the mess and quickly pinned the diaper up again. The stench hung in the air.

"Jolene," he called, thinking maybe his energy would go outside to her and she'd know to come home. Women's intuition and all that. Dandy began to crawl around and Artie wagged his finger at him, because he knew that was something parents did when they were in charge and wanted to make a point. "You drop piss or shit on the floor and you can work the sponge yourself."

He lifted the shopping bag to the table. Dandy sat in front of the stove, and Artie grabbed the present he'd bought—a red rubber ball—and handed it to Dandy. The kid smiled and dropped it.

Artie gave it back to Dandy and told him to take good care of it. But Dandy pushed the ball away again. "Look, if you ain't gonna appreciate it, I'll keep it myself." He put the ball in the crook of Dandy's legs. Dandy groped for it and pushed it away once more. Artie was getting mad fast. "I ain't got all day to play with you," he said.

He snatched up the ball and squeezed it. "You want to play a game, huh? I'll teach you a game." He zipped the ball into Dandy's stomach. Dandy gave an "oof" and his face bunched up in surprise. The ball bounced away and Artie threw it again. It thumped against Dandy's chest and he started to cry. What am I doing? Artie thought. He's just a kid. He placed the ball gently in Dandy's hands. "Don't aggravate me now, I got enough to worry about with your mother," he said.

Dandy brought the ball to his mouth and tried to gnaw on it, but it was too big.

Artie lit a cigarette and sat at the table smoking and watching the light darken in the room. When Dandy fell asleep, he lifted the kid into his box and covered him with the towel. He could use a nap himself, Artie thought. When he saw how clean the bedroom was, he felt at his clothes. They were stiff with dirt.

He shuffled into the bathroom and filled the tub. While the water was running he took the whiskey out of the shopping bag. He had been planning on saving it and opening it up for the two of them, making a big show, saying it was their anniversary—he didn't know if it was or not; she wouldn't know either. But what the hell, he thought. It wasn't his fault she wasn't here. Anyways, taking a bath was a special occasion too. He cracked the cap.

It always surprised him, how much he enjoyed sitting in a hot tub of water. It was like a spiritual experience. It reminded him of the way he felt in church on Christmas Eve, the one time a year he attended. He always swore he could actually feel God there. Once, in the ninth grade, he almost fainted during the service. There seemed to be something scrambling in his lungs and he decided to ask the priest, old fat Father DiCicco, what it was all about. He hung around after Mass, waiting for the parishioners to leave, and stopped the priest on the cobblestone sidewalk in front of the church. They halted beside a butcher shop, where skinned, gutted lambs hung from metal hooks in the display window, dripping blood onto wax paper. Artie remembered it as if it were yesterday.

"You were filled with the spirit," Father DiCicco told him. "It was God telling you you're a special person. He has a special mission for you." Artie liked that idea. He thought that must be it. He was supposed to be a priest, or a bishop, maybe even Pope.

He went to church the next week and pretended it was the same. He kept waiting to faint, looking for weird feelings in his chest, thinking maybe they were there but he didn't recognize them. By the third week, though, he couldn't keep still in his seat long enough to listen to what the priest was talking about. All Artie cared about was checking out the girls. Since then, he'd done all his religion on Christmas Eve.

He knew a bath was like that. You had to be away from it long enough to forget what it was like before you could really appreciate it. He slid low, so his ears were beneath the waterline. The heat of the water and splash of sound pressed in on him. It felt so good he ran more hot water, to keep the temperature up. He used the soap, his eyes closed tight while he lathered and rubbed. When he opened them the water was such a dark gray it startled him. That can't really be me, he thought. He pulled the plug. He stepped out, keeping his back to it. It had to be the dirt from the tub.

He toweled off and thought about the bath and church. Being with Jolene was like that too. A tenderness rolled around inside his chest. It wasn't until he was away from her that he appreciated what she meant to him. He felt happier and closer to her, and more frightened, than ever in his life. He wished she were there right that moment, before the good feeling wore off. He wanted to share it with her before he lost it. He knew feelings like that only lasted a short time.

The chill in the air made him shiver, and he moved to the stove, cranked up the gas log, and kneeled before it for warmth. "If I could just get a start somehow," he said softly to Dandy. "I could make her happy."

He went into the bedroom for some clothes. He didn't want to put his dirty clothes back on, and he didn't know if he had any clean ones. He figured, if it came to that, he could wear something of hers around the house. As long as nobody saw, what difference did it make? He slid open the closet.

On the floor in the corner his dogs were jumbled in a pile as if they'd been dumped from a toybox. He picked out one that had a broken ear. There were other broken things . . . ears, tails, paws, noses. He had to wipe roughly at his eyes with the heel of his hand to stop himself from crying. Goddamn, what was wrong with people? He sat with his feet beneath him. Nobody understood, he thought. Not even Jolene. He sunk his hands into the pile and moved his fingers through it gently. The soft clinking of the dogs was saying something to him. But what? he waited for clarity.

Then he heard the footsteps, the pause at the landing. He had just enough time to push everything back into the closet, run to the kitchen, wrap on the neck brace, and press its Velcro clasp together. Then her hand hit the doorknob.

# CHAPTER
# —16—

He forgot about being naked until she opened the door and the cold from the hallway hit him. There was nothing to do about it, though. Not now. Goose bumps spread across his arms and he started shivering. He smiled nervously. "Energy," he told her. He made a few spastic movements with his arms to show her that's what it was, not the cold.

"What're you doing naked? Where's my baby? What have you done to him?" Her body was stiff, but her voice animated. She stood beyond the threshold.

"Hey, whoa—he's in bed, sleeping. I haven't done nothing." He motioned toward the box in the corner.

"Why don't you have clothes on?"

"I just took a bath." He smiled. "I wanted to be clean and new for you, gal."

"Did you do anything to Dandy? You better tell me."

"What are you talking about?"

She looked him up and down, then looked away.

"Do what?"

She shook her head as if apologizing before stepping into the room, shutting the door, and leaning back against it. Her hands were in her coat pockets and her head tipped sideways. She looked pretty fine, he thought, in the boots and the green dress. Green being his favorite color. But she had a nothing look on her face; her eyes reflected the room like blank TV screens.

"What are you looking for?" she asked him. Her voice wasn't angry, just matter-of-fact, and that threw him off.

Suddenly he felt embarrassed, and he held his hands together before him, to cover up.

"Well," she said. "You better hurry up and state your business."

"Just give me a minute here," Artie said. He kept one hand in front of his crotch and raised the other in a plea for silence. His throat felt jittery, but he had to give it a shot. He counted four, snapping his fingers on each beat, then began to sing. "I'm gonna make you love meeee." He hopped to the right, then to the left, right, left—kicking one foot out and clapping his hands on each beat, four to the measure. He had to keep his body stiff because of the neck brace. "Yes I will, yes I wi-i-i-iiiil. I'm gonna make you love meeee."

Jolene looked like she could laugh or cry, go either way. But it wasn't enough, she was still holding back. He stopped singing. Hit her with something practical, he told himself, before she had a chance to think.

"Look at this," he said. He pointed directly at her, then turned to the shopping bag. He held up the items while he listed them. "I got some potatoes we can bake, I got us one can of tunafish, I got a paper—I mean, how can we be a regular family if we ain't got a newspaper to read when we come home at night? And look at the stories in this—I mean, hell, they're so interesting you'll probably want to read them twice." He pointed at the headline: MOTHER CHOPS UP TWO-HEADED BABY. She didn't seem real enthused. He set the paper down and pulled out the whiskey. "Remember this?" he said. "You know how people talk about 'our song'? Well, this is 'our bottle.' This is the stuff we got the first day I moved in." He hugged it to his chest before holding it out to her. She kept staring, not moving, not saying anything. It gave him the creeps. Even if she yelled, that was something he could relate to. It'd give him something to work with. "You know what else I got you?" It was his last card, but it was a good one. "Now, it's only on account of you deserve it." He pulled from the bag half a dozen soggy packages of boil-in-the-pouch Salisbury steaks. "Steaks." Water dripped down his arms and splatted on the floor. He put them on the table with the rest of the groceries and pulled out two more handfuls. Then two more. "I got us enough we can eat steak every single meal for a month. Now what do you say to that, huh?"

She didn't budge.

He listened to the traffic sounds outside and the loud noise of his own breathing. Something had to give. He'd shot his wad. She reached into her pocket, and for a second he was certain she was going to pull a gun on him. "Wait a minute now," he said, and stepped backward, into the stove.

She pulled out a pack of Camels, shook one out, took it between her lips, and stared at the floor. Her head shook slightly from side to side. She raised the pack toward her face and poked the cigarette back into it.

"Well now," Artie said. "Ha ha." The bag was ripping through at the bottom from the wetness of the thawed steaks, but he folded it and looked for a place to store it. He wedged it between Dandy's box and the stove. He should've got something personal for her. He knew he'd forgotten something. He should've picked up a present she could have just for herself. Tampons or something. The rubber ball was on the floor before him, and he picked it up. "I wanted to get you something special too," he said, tossing the ball in one hand. "But I spent every penny I had on this." It wasn't really a lie. He didn't have any *change* left. The ball hit the ceiling and fell beyond his reach. It bounced across the floor toward Jolene. She stopped it with her boot. "A little something for your kid," Artie said.

She looked up sharply. "You bought Dandy a present?"

He started to shrug it off, then he opened out his arms and smiled. "Hey, that kid's like my own boy. I mean, everybody has their problems, but I ain't going to hold nothing against him. I mean, Jolene now, I got to set an example, right?"

She rolled the ball back and forth beneath her foot. "I don't want no one-time thing, Artie. If you're coming back, it's got to be something that moves along. One step goes to another. We got to get someplace."

He took a step closer, but she stopped him with a look. He thought she was just talking, but she acted like what she said meant something to her. "What place do you want to get to?" he asked.

"I want to get to the place where . . . where, all of us, Dandy too, do things together. Like . . . like . . . I don't know. Go to the zoo and feed the animals."

"What do you want to see animals for?" he said. "You got me. You can feed me. I mean, let's make sense here."

"Artie, it's not the zoo. It's the *us*." She kicked the ball away and looked toward the window. Her breath came out in a short, cold huff.

"Oh, right, yeah," he said, nodding his head. "I see your point. Sure. We can go to the zoo. We can go to the dog races. Anywhere."

"Us too," she said. "We got to get ourselves into something official."

He wanted to sit down and think about that one awhile, but he was afraid, if he sat, his skin might stick to the plastic cushion on the chair.

"Don't expect me to beg you to stay," she said, looking over at him. "I'm not doing anything like that."

"Beg nothing." There seemed to be all kinds of feelings floating around. Most of them were unclear, but he guessed somehow that she was giving in. "Give me your coat," he said. She looked confused as he moved over and held her collar, like a real gentleman, while she pulled her arms from the sleeves. She grabbed the coat back from him and took a paper bag from the pocket. She set it on the table and tossed the coat to Artie. He could tell there was a bottle inside the bag, and he gave her a quick eye, to let her know she wasn't putting anything over on him. He didn't say anything, though. No sense getting off the track just yet.

When he put her coat on the floor she started to squawk. He didn't want to yell back at her so he put his hands to his ears and shook his head. "I ain't listening," he said. He put his knees down on the coat and when she tried to pull it out from under him he hunched lower to cover more of the material. "Trust me, now, come on, trust me." She stepped back and put her hands on her hips. He wished he had a hard-on. It'd make for a better effect, he thought. He talked to his penis in his mind, but it did no good and he decided he couldn't wait. Giving her his full smile, he pulled his hands together, palm to palm, fingers pointing up. "Jolene, I'm the one down here, on my knees, just throwing my pride on the garbage heap. But I'm willing to take all the blame, even if it ain't mine—that's okay, that's all right, that's what men are for." He knew he had to look serious in this part, but he felt so good being in the same room with her again, things looking up and all, he couldn't help smiling. "Well, what do you say, gal? Huh? What about it?"

"What about what?"

"Do I have to spell it out?" he asked. "Jeez, give me a break." He sang one more chorus, moving his torso stiffly from side to side. "I'm gonna make you love meeeeeee."

She worked a curl behind her ear with one hand and looked away. She stared around the kitchen, puffed out a breath, and stared at him again. "Why do I even bother listening to you?" She looked at him with the sad, foggy eyes of someone who'd already quit, but who didn't know it yet.

"Because we have a blast together," he said. "Dancing, drinking, eating. Raising up the little whippersnapper." He bounced excitedly. "Gal, oooooh. You get me all hepped up."

His smile was real and so big it hurt his cheeks. But she didn't move. It was like she wasn't all there.

He was starting to get nervous. He didn't want to lose her. That made him want to tell the truth seriously, which scared him. "Jolene," he said, unable to stop himself, "I . . . well, you know . . . I—well, sort of, I guess—I like—like you." He closed his eyes and knew it was true. "I love you." He put his hands to the floor for balance. Looking up, he said in a soft voice, "God-damn it, gal, what more do you want from me? I'm sorry for all the problems. I just want things to be smooth again."

A smile opened slowly on her face. She looked like she was going to cry. He pressed his head against her abdomen and closed his eyes. She smelled warm through the fabric of her dress. Something about that, and the way she ran her fingers through his hair like she was trying to keep him away from something, made him feel like crying himself. He'd never been so terrified in his life.

There was a scuffling sound, then the ripe odor of shit filled the air. Dandy was standing up, jiggling in his box.

"Oh Dandy, you stink," Jolene said, stepping back from Artie and pinching her nose. "Oh baby why do you need to be changed *now?* God, that's the last thing I want to do."

"I'll change him," Artie said, and he felt like he'd been slapped. The shock in his own face reflected the surprise in Jolene's.

"You can do that?" she asked.

"Of course I can *do* it. Anybody can *do* it." He was in it now, he thought. No turning back. "I want to do it for you, Jolene." He stood up, set his hands in Dandy's armpits, lifted him from the floor, and held him at arm's length. "Just this once." He turned him around and looked at the bulging diaper. "But maybe he wants to be changed by his mother," he said.

"Let me hang up my coat," she said. "This I have to see."

His eyes danced around the kitchen, looking for an escape hatch, as she went into the bedroom.

When she reentered the kitchen she was momentarily confused. It was empty. The toilet flushed and she turned to the bathroom. He can't be, she thought. Not really. She pushed open the door and Artie looked up at her, giving her a sudden smile meant to calm and reassure her.

"Now listen," he said. "I know how this looks, but give me a chance to explain." Dandy's diaper was on the floor by his feet and Artie held the boy over the toilet bowl. He dunked him, then set him in the path of the rushing water, angling him around to hit all the spots. "This is the latest in modern science," Artie told Jolene.

"Artie," she said, horrified, but trying not to laugh.

"I ain't lying, Jolene. I'm telling you. It's in all the newspapers. Probably on TV too. They do this in Europe all the time. The old country ways, you know? They've done all these studies on it to show it's the best thing you can do for your kid. See? Clean as new." He displayed Dandy's bottom for her approval. His legs were all red with rash. Artie said, "I'm telling you, gal, it's the latest rage. They been doing this for centuries and they ain't lost one kid yet. It's the best way to get rid of the germs, you know? It keeps you clean, keeps the kid clean, there's no need to bother wiping—and think of the money you save." He lifted Dandy's face to his own. "Don't you feel better? Tell your mama how Uncle Artie takes care of you."

Dandy looked pained, the skin on his face all folds and ridges. An arc of urine shot from his penis and hit Artie's bare foot.

Artie watched the pee dribble to a small pool on the floor. "Oh man, I just had a bath," he said. He turned to Jolene. In that moment, Artie looked as helpless as Dandy did.

"Oh Artie," Jolene said, and she started to laugh.

They put Dandy in his box and spread a blanket on the kitchen floor. Artie went down on Jolene, working on her with the rough eagerness of a stray dog brought food. She moaned and shook when she came and he crawled up, hooked her knees onto his shoulders, and slid inside, pumping rapidly. She urged him on with cries of "Harder, harder." He flipped her onto her stomach and used his hand on her clitoris until she came again. Then he stood her up, bent her over the table, and took her in the ass. They went back to the floor and he thrust into her from the side until he came. Then they started all over again.

An hour later they were stretched in front of the stove, head to foot, panting, the blanket damp and the smell of sex a heavy mist in the air. Their bodies were smeared with sweat.

In Artie's eyes, Jolene's body seemed to fade into the slate light filling the kitchen. There was a purple glow on her face from the gas flame on the side of the stove. He put the neck brace back on and lay still, resting.

A sound like meat hitting a counter startled them. On the floor Dandy was stretched flat, and whimpering. Jolene lifted one arm feebly, then let it fall again.

"Look at that," Artie said. He grabbed Dandy by one arm and slid him closer. "The kid's got balls. He climbed right out of that box and made it safe between the chair legs." Dandy crawled out from under Artie's hand and moved between him and Jolene. "Wait a minute here," Artie said. "No one muscles in on my territory." Dandy settled his head against Artie's side. He had stopped crying. He was kind of warm, too, against Artie's skin.

"Where you been, Artie?"

"You kicked me out, remember?"

"Things wouldn't have happened."

"What things?" She'd turned into the room and he couldn't make out her face anymore. He tucked Dandy in closer to himself. He didn't know about this here.

She rolled to a sitting position. "Artie, I'm sorry, I didn't even ask how you are." She looked at him and laughed. "You look like Frankenstein, that's why I'm laughing. I'm sorry." She caressed his stitches.

"I ain't no monster, now," he told her. "My head's just fucked up."

She leaned forward and kissed him. He hugged her for a while. When she sat back he touched the neck brace with both hands.

"Honey, what's wrong with your neck? Is it serious?"

He looked at her huddled form. "Well, now, that's a story. Get me a drink, Jolene, I don't want to wake up the mountain climber here." He patted Dandy. "You know, that wouldn't be a bad idea. If we could get this kid to climb Mount Everest or something. You know? The youngest kid to climb a mountain. People'd be wanting autographs and books. We'd be on the talk shows. People'd be watching us on TV. We could make us some serious money. What do you think?"

Jolene came back with the bottle. She helped him sit up and pour down some whiskey. "Ah the pain," he said as he lay back down. "It's all right, Jolene. It's not your fault you don't know how to handle me. It's okay. Let me just rest a second, make sure the shrapnel didn't shift closer to my major nerves and arteries." He breathed deeply. It was pleasant—Dandy warming his side, Jolene's hand hot on his chest, the whiskey shooting feelers from his stomach to his brain. This is the life, he thought. If it could go on forever he'd be all set. He went over the last few days in his mind, recalling them clearly. Every second was there, it seemed. He told the full story to himself and decided which parts he'd tell Jolene.

"It all started," he began, "when I was working on the engine. Trying to get it fixed so I could come for you, so I could make sure you were all right. Rescue you, you know?"

"Honey, really?"

"Sure. No telling what might've happened to you, without me there to take care of you." He looked at Jolene. She had a look on her face that he knew about. It was a lot of things, but mostly guilt.

"I had just finished it too," he said. "I'm standing there, freezing cold, my fingers ready to fall off from frostbite, just about ready to pull my head out, when from nowhere this must've-been-twenty-wheeler trailer truck comes bombing at me and smashes into Smitty's car. 'Course, the hood snaps down on my neck and the car goes tearing forward and here I am—my head stuck, my feet moving just barely fast enough to keep up, and you know what I'm thinking? I'm thinking, If my head gets ripped off, how am I ever going to explain things to Jolene?"

Jolene gave a laugh and Artie looked at her so she'd settle down, know it was serious.

"'Course, really, I was mostly worried about you." She leaned closer. "I knew how you'd be, knowing it was all your fault, me sitting on the side of the road with blood pumping out this hole between my shoulders like I was a fire hydrant or something. You know how that made me feel? Knowing you'd be carrying around that guilt with you the rest of your life for what you'd done to me? It made me feel terrible, and I decided I wasn't going to die—for your sake."

She laid her head on his chest. Artie touched her hair. He was amazed at how it could all be there, everything that had happened to him, his life, so clear it wasn't even like his life. It was like a movie. The best part, though was that he could keep it a secret. All for himself. He could tell the story any way he wanted and who would know? He could tell her about the brain operation and the nurse wanting to marry him and how, with the shrapnel, one false move and it was curtains for him. He could tell her all these things.

Who could say it wasn't real?

# CHAPTER —17—

They talked and laughed and made love desperately, as if proving and cleansing themselves, as if they were fearful it wouldn't last. They swore love constantly, back and forth, until saying "I love you" came as naturally as breathing and nearly as often. Their only arguments were about who loved the other more. Each of them claimed that honor, and they'd bicker about it, laughing up to an hour at a time.

They didn't need to go out. They had the whiskey and each other and enough food. The ate Salisbury steak for eight meals in a row letting Dandy share it, too. Both of them were sick of it finally, but neither wanted to say anything for fear of hurting the other's feelings. As they settled down to yet another supper of hamburger and gravy, they both sat with poised forks, smiling, passing the bottle, neither making a move for the food. Then Artie stood up. "Hey, this is our three-day anniversary, three days since we got back together. It calls for something special. Let me take you out, Jolene, and we'll do it up right."

"Thank God," she said. She stood up and went straight to the door. They didn't even put the food in the refrigerator.

They went to a Kentucky Fried Chicken and ordered nine pieces, cole slaw, potato salad, and two Cokes, which Artie held under the table and spilled whiskey into. While they ate he kept looking at her, chuckling, then looking away. "What? What are you laughing about?" she asked him repeatedly. But he'd only shake his head and smile.

"You'll see," he told her.

"I'll see what? Artie?"

"Just eat your food, we'll talk later."

When they were finished he piled all the bones and the empty cole slaw and potato salad cups inside the red and white box the chicken had come in. He cleared that and the Coke cans off to the side of the white plastic tabletop. "I been thinking things over the past few days." He wiped his hands with the last napkin, then rubbed them on his pants. "Now close your eyes."

She waited, excited, trying to peek, but he was watching her. "All the way shut or you ain't getting nothing," he told her. She shut them tight and clasped her hands on the tabletop. He placed one hand over hers, then wedged his hand in between so he could hold her left hand with his. "Okay, you can look now," he said. In his right hand he held the ring tops to the two Coke cans.

"Now, this ain't nothing but the idea, you know? It's nothing set yet, so we can still get out of it." He dropped one of the ring tops into her right palm. "It goes all right, as soon as we get some cash, we'll do it up proper. City Hall, Cold Duck—the whole nine yards." He lifted her hand and slid the tab onto her ring finger. Then he held out his left hand for her to do the same. His hand was shaking so bad it took her some time to slide the tab on. They stared at each other for a while, holding and squeezing each other's fingers. She expected to hear bands playing in her head, or something, but they were insulated in an overwhelming silence. Artie looked as though he was on the edge between unbounded terror and glee.

"Are you sure about this, Artie?" Jolene asked.

"Are you saying I ain't man enough to make this kind of decision?"

"No no no, honey. Relax now. I didn't mean nothing like that. It's just—it surprised me, that's all." She touched his face, and he turned his lips to kiss her palm.

"Hey, I been thinking, you know? You got to start somewhere. And I know this is what you really want. I don't mind. I mean, you can still get out of it if you want. If you change your mind."

"Oh no no nooooo. I'll never do that."

He looked down at the table. "Nobody wants to get stuck alone, right? And it's even better 'cause we love each other." He lifted his eyes to her face. "Jolene darling, now we can take care of each other. Work together, you know? We'll figure out something." He touched at the neck brace.

She reached up to hold his face with both hands, but he grabbed her left wrist and showed her the flat edge of the tab where it'd been broken from the can. "You got to be careful, that thing can make me bleed." She put her right hand behind his head and pulled him close over the table for a long, wet kiss.

"All right. Let's get plastered," he said. "Let's get bombed. Let's get so loaded we can't remember our own names. I'm talking serious celebration here. Drinking, dancing—" He moved in his seat with an imaginary dance partner. "Let's go to 'our bar.'"

Her breath choked up in her throat and she tried not to show him her fears. "Let's go home, honey, I just want to be with you alone tonight."

"Hell, I ain't going to be with no one but you on that dance floor. We got plenty of time for being alone on our honeymoon." He stood and reached for her hand. "Nothing to worry about there. Where do you want to do the honeymoon, anyways? I was figuring someplace nice, like Buzzard's Bay." He held his left hand aloft and seemed genuinely happy. "Ah, this makes me feel like a new man. For better and worse. Rich and poor. All that stuff. Fat and thin, death and life." He walked her out into the night. She held his arm, but it didn't help. She felt like she was walking down a long, ill-lit tunnel.

It looked like a science fiction movie, she thought: the darkness, neon signs, one streetlight in the middle spreading a blue surface over the pocked road. A thin fog drifted down the street and women seemed to walk with it, as if they were a part of the mist. Their faces were white with makeup, their eyes starkly outlined in black. Red slashes of blush showed on their cheeks like bruises. The women seemed to watch Jolene closely as she passed them, hugging tight to Artie. "Don't worry," he told her. "They don't interest me no more." He patted her hand.

It was packed inside Charley's. "All these dressed-up guys," Artie said, hanging just inside the door. "Must be a convention in town." He took a step into the crowd and bobbed his head, looking for the best way to the back. There was a hooting, grunting sound in the place, of people ready to let go but still holding themselves back. The sound reminded Jolene of animal shows, the jungle at night. She felt they were all looking at her, showing her their eyeballs, teeth, tongues, making slight motions with their hands and mouths. Most of them were dressed up and looked respectable, except for the hyena snarls on their faces.

She looked above their heads, where the smoke rose in distinct layers. A woman in her fifties with a platinum wig and sagging breasts and stomach danced to a disco song in the orange light on the runway behind the bar. She snapped her sequined panties off and Jolene was shocked to see that she had shaved off her pubic hair. Laughter dominoed around the near curve of the bar and someone yelled, "Put it back on." The woman gave the guy the finger and stalked back down the runway to disappear behind bead curtains and purple drapery.

"A little action tonight, huh?" Artie said. He hopped up and kissed her on the cheek. "Don't it feel good?" His eyes shone as he looked around the place. There were so many people, there didn't appear to be a path through the crowd. He breathed in deeply. "Nothing like a little energy to get the old juices flowing." He squeezed her hand. "C'mon, let's weasel our way to the back."

He took two steps before Jolene saw the black woman. She recognized Jolene right away. She slammed her drink down onto the bar and started pushing her way through the crowd, shoving men out of her path, to get to Jolene. A hard, glassy-eyed stare took over the woman's face and Jolene's stomach seemed to fall through her legs, past her thighs and calves. Artie grabbed Jolene's hand and stepped forward, but was snapped back when she didn't move. "What's the problem?" he asked.

She couldn't answer. He turned just as Jolene worked her hand loose from his, and then the woman was upon them.

"You goddamned motherfucker," the black woman screamed,

punching Jolene in the face. Jolene staggered backward and the woman pressed forward, pushing her toward the door. Artie was caught in the middle between their bodies and the punches, and he moved with them, covering his head with his arms.

Jolene swung back wildly, the woman blocking with her forearms. She pushed Jolene in the chest and reached around with one arm to grab the hair at the back of Jolene's head. She yanked it back and they slammed into the door, wrestling and pulling at each other. Artie slipped loose and yelled, "What the fuck? What the fuck?" He pulled on the woman's arms, but she kept pushing and punching at Jolene. Then she grabbed her by the coat and, leaning her full weight into it, slammed Jolene against the door so hard it banged open and the three of them tumbled out into the cement foyer. Jolene was on the bottom, trying to hold the woman's arms. Artie got up from the ground and grabbed the woman's Afro with both hands. He pulled her sideways. She was half off when a thin white man with a goatee and eyes like balled mercury glided up to Artie. Jolene saw a brief silver glinting as the man made a stabbing motion at Artie's arm. Artie howled like a dog hit by a car. He glanced at the man, then clambered over the two women onto the sidewalk, ready to run. Jolene saw his pants darken and she knew he had wet himself.

The black woman looked back at the man with the knife and said, "This the bitch thinks she's gonna work my territory." In the doorway of the bar men's faces, openmouthed with excitement, stared out at them.

The man with the goatee pointed his knife at Artie and said, "Fucking Frankie the Weasel's kid—what do you think, you're in the big time?" He pointed the blade at Jolene and told Artie, "Get your ugly motherfucking piece of ass out of here. And if I ever see you around, I'm gonna cut your fucking balls off." He nodded once to the black woman and she leaned back, away from Jolene's face.

Jolene let go of the black woman's arms and the woman slapped her twice hard across the face. "You crawl in one more motherfucking car on this street, honey, and I'll cut your motherfucking pussy out." She stood up and kicked Jolene in the side. Jolene cried out and turned to Artie, but he was holding his arm, watching the knife, backing into the street. His lips trembled. His whole body shook. He looked like a little boy. Jolene felt so bad for what she'd done to him, she wished she could die.

The man stepped forward and kicked Jolene in the ass. "Get the fuck out of here. Don't you understand English?" She stumbled to her feet, crawling on her hands to get up and away from him, and without looking back she started running.

She ran with Artie beside her. He was trying to watch over his shoulder, but the neck brace got in his way. Halfway down the street he unsnapped it and let it drop.

"Honey, your neck, the shrapnel," she said. He wouldn't look at her.

They made it to the corner, saw no one was following them, and stopped, gasping. "Are you all right? Are you all right? Let me see," she said, her words heaving out. She touched his hand where it clutched his wounded arm. "Honey, are you hurt bad? Should we go to the hospital?" The buildings swayed around her.

He looked at the cut through his coat, then at his hand, at the slick darkness of the blood on his fingers. "I'm bleeding," he said, and started to cry.

He turned from her and she tried to come around to face him. But he kept turning. She felt like she was chasing someone on a merry-go-round. They spun in a circle on the corner, the yellow, pink, and white light from the theater marquee across the street casting garish stripes on their faces as they passed through it, turned around, and passed again. "Honey," Jolene said over and over. "Honey . . . honey . . . honey."

"Leave me alone!" he screamed. "Just leave me alone. Leave me alone." They were both crying, their voices ragged. It sounded like he was trying to make himself stop but couldn't. She wondered how they could ever get over this. What could she possibly do to make things right again? It wasn't fair, she thought. Just when things were starting to get straight. Couldn't they get a break anywhere?

"Please let me help you," she said.

"Like I helped you."

"Honey, please." She wiped his face with her fingertips.

"Don't look at me," he told her, turning away again. "Leave me alone."

She grabbed his good arm and stopped him. "Please, let me, please help you."

He stared at her face, then looked away. His left hand touched briefly at the front of his pants. "What do you want me to say?" He was crying so hard he shook. Taking her hand, he pressed it to his groin. She snapped it away in revulsion. "See?" he said. "You happy now?" He spun away from her again.

People in passing cars slowed and stared. Occasionally they beeped their horns. "It's all right," she told him. "It don't matter." She continued moving around with him, trying to look into his face. Finally he grew dizzy and staggered to a halt against a building.

He looked at his wound. "Goddamn me," he said, lifting his hand and watching a few drops of blood drip to the sidewalk. "Goddamn." Each syllable was choked out on a sob. "I don't even know the first thing this is about. You got something to tell me about this?"

The jittering made it feel like her face was falling into little pieces. Something shifted beneath Jolene's feet and she looked down, waiting for the sidewalk to rip open. Her mind seemed to expand, to connect with the block: the buildings, the sidewalk, the streets, the ruts, the signs, the odors—she latched on, became a part of them in her head and in some distant, unlocated center her self diminished to a single strand of concern for Artie.

She knew, somehow, she'd have to explain it all. She knew payments would have to be made. There was a soft tick and she looked down to see the ring tab on the sidewalk by Artie's feet. It looked like it had always been there.

# CHAPTER
# —18—

He wouldn't go to the hospital. He'd done that once, and he figured if he went back again, he'd be jinxed. It wasn't that deep anyways, and had pretty much stopped bleeding by the time they got back to the apartment. There weren't any Band-Aids, so after washing the cut out with a facecloth, Jolene tied a knee sock around his arm to catch the blood. As she worked she told him everything. She wouldn't look at him as she explained, and he was thankful for that. It felt like he'd been knocked into a hole and people were shoveling dirt on him.

He left the kitchen without a word. Passing the bathroom, he looked in to see his dungarees hanging over the shower curtain bar, right next to Dandy's diapers. She'd rinsed them and wrung them out for him, and now there was a puddle of faint blue water on the linoleum. The pants were still dripping and the water crept in a thin rivulet toward the kitchen. Artie shut the bathroom door. He didn't need no reminders.

"Don't just walk away, honey, please say something." Jolene's voice was a wind at his back. "Yell at me, anything," she said.

He bent to the mattress, then covered himself with the blanket. He had to face toward the door so he wouldn't lie on his wounded arm. He curled up with his knees close to his chest. He didn't know which was worse, what he hadn't done or what she had done. He tried to tell himself that at least he hadn't run away. That was something. But it wasn't much, because he would've run if he'd been able to move his feet. His breaths reverberated, the sound magnified in his ears. Unseen forces seemed to gather in long thin clouds, rushing and pausing all around the room.

"Artie," Jolene said from the doorway. The word echoed. *Ar-tie-tie-tie-tie-tie.* He was incapable of movement. He couldn't even tell her to shut up.

She knelt beside him and spoke in earnest, plaintive tones, holding his hand between hers and lifting it to her mouth to kiss his fingers every few seconds. He tried not to listen, to distance himself from her touch. It came to him then, a slow understanding unfolding in his mind. The thing with explanations is they don't matter. They don't help. It's just one more reminder that you've been fucked over again.

"Please don't be hurt. Please, Artie. Oh honey, it breaks my heart to see you like this. You're never quiet. Please, just say something. Tell me I'm evil. Honey? It scares me to see you like this."

She bent down and tried to look directly into his eyes, but he wouldn't let her have them. He was in a faraway place, and he didn't want to come back. He wouldn't. What was left for him?

She stood and he watched her ankles walk from view. He heard a television set snap on in the apartment below them. He wished he were inside that set, so someone could switch the channel and make him not be there anymore. The volume was loud at first, but after a minute someone turned it down until it became a barely audible hum. The dry hiss of cars called to him from outside. He swore he smelled things, faint salty odors, that didn't belong to him or to Jolene. He shifted on the bed. Odd lumps and indentations hit his body, as if the mattress had been conforming to someone else's shape. He didn't know what she'd done exactly—she hadn't told him the particulars—but in his mind he saw a vision of Jolene in the middle of a pit like the Wrangler's, Jell-O smeared on her naked body, stars of light shining through the darkness of the club; and all around her, standing shoulder to shoulder around the pit, were well-dressed men, suits and ties, shiny shoes, neat haircuts and close-shaven faces. They all had their zippers down and were waiting for their turn.

He closed his eyes and moved his legs. His groin and thigh felt slightly sticky and he thought he caught the sour scent of urine.

The closet door made a scratchy, rattling sound as it opened. He heard the chinking of his dogs, then the mattress jounced as Jolene dropped onto it. Artie opened his eyes to the face of Lucky, his stuffed dog, and he reached out impulsively and grabbed it. He pulled it under the covers and raised the blanket to look at it. "My old man gave me this for my fifth birthday," he said. Jolene was sitting with her feet beneath her and her hands on the tops of her legs. "I used to bring it to school with me, keep it in my desk, you know?" He turned the head back and forth, pretending to himself that it was alive. He was losing control again and he squeezed his eyes with one hand. "Can you cut the light, Jolene?"

She snapped it off and dropped to the mattress again. He looked at her, relieved that she couldn't see him clearly. The light from the kitchen entered the room in a dim, fanlike spray, outlining her left side. Her right side seemed in the process of dissolving.

"Some goddamn kids—" His voice caught. He remembered the day, getting a bathroom pass and leaving the classroom. He was in the second grade, the first time around. When he returned, he found the dog's head stuck in his inkwell and the body inside the desk, the fabric ripped apart and the stuffing scattered in small gray clots all over his crayons and paints. "My old man says, What the fuck's the sense in buying you anything, you can't take care of it? Take care of it. I was seven years old. He should fucking talk. He left that year. Know what he told me? Opportunity knocks. Nothing else . . . seven years old and he said, Opportunity knocks. Fuck him. Maybe he ain't even my father." He felt the fabric of the dog's head. It was matted and grimy. There was a point here somewhere, he thought. But goddamn if he knew what it was.

"I don't understand, honey," Jolene said.

"Goddamn it! You can't let nothing count too much," he yelled. "It's . . . you got to get them before they get you." He looked at her, then away. "Everyone's waiting for you." He was confused. "I don't know what the fuck I'm talking about. But you ain't helping me. Stop staring!" He was crying suddenly and Jolene was over him, her fingers and lips gently moving over his face. He rolled away, onto his back. He felt lost, unconnected to the world. "I'm just penny ante," he told the ceiling, looking at the cracks and flakes just visible in the seeping spread of light.

"You're not penny ante, Artie." She stretched beside him, speaking close to his ear so the words came into his head warm and damp.

"What do you call it?" His voice was harsh and thick. "Purses, B and Es, old ladies and little kids—I once robbed four kids at a bus stop, you know that? It's nickel-and-dime stuff, Jolene. I'm nickel-and-dime stuff. I ain't never going to amount to nothing. What the hell am I?" He looked at the dog's head in his hand and threw it across the room. It thudded against the window and hit the floor with a soft *thup*.

Jolene put her hand to his chest. "What you done—at least you never killed no one," she said. "You're not penny ante to me."

"What do you know? You're just penny ante too. We're both of us taking these little goddamn steps and we ain't going nowhere. The ground's moving away faster than we can get our feet down." A pressure pushed against the skin of his face; it felt like his head was squeezed into a small round ball. "If I had killed somebody, at least I'd know where I was in this world." Her hand lifted off his chest and moved away. He looked at her sorrowful face. From the kitchen Dandy gave out an angry "Na na na." That was followed by a short scraping sound. "What about him? What the hell's he got ahead of him?" Artie raised himself up on one arm and hollered, "Stay in your box, you're better off."

"We'll think of something, Artie," Jolene said.

"Think of something? You got to be a goddamn Einstein to figure things out in this world."

"Maybe we can get jobs and save up our money." Her hands were on his forearms and she gripped him tightly.

"Man, Jolene. What am I going to do? Sit in a factory? I been on the streets too long. I won't take to no leash. I never fit in nowhere. I never—"

"Artie, calm down, please, honey."

"I never belonged no place. I could never do nothing. It's too late now to start. Jolene, I'm telling you—"

"Artie, please don't get yourself upset."

"Upset? What the hell do you know? What happened here tonight? What happened here and what you just told me? 'Don't get upset.' I'm trying to talk to you, trying to tell you that nothing's ever going to happen for me in my life, that we ain't never going to get out of this shit; I could fucking kill you."

He found himself leaning over her with both hands pressed to her shoulders near her neck. He pulled back, lifted his hands, and turned to face the window, a dark sheet reflecting unclear images. The bed rustled as she shifted. He felt her cold damp hand on his back, moving up to rub his neck.

"Honey," she said, "there has got to be something we can do. We'll figure out something. Maybe we should just pack up and go somewhere far away, start over. I read a newspaper in the laundromat telling a story about down south, I think. There's a place called the Sunbelt. I guess it's always shining and there are jobs and ways to make a living. Opportunities. That's what it said. People like us are moving there because of all the opportunities. Maybe we can find us one."

"It takes money to get an opportunity," he told her.

"I know," she said, her voice moving away. "We'll figure something out." She pulled him onto his back and slowly began to rub his penis.

She worked on him for a long time. She tried everything, and kept telling him, "It don't matter, that's all right." She touched him lightly and when that didn't work she squeezed him until he hurt. When that didn't work either she took him in her mouth and sucked on him, then tried using just her tongue softly on his cap. She rolled on top of him and ground against him. She told him that didn't matter either. If he believed her, nothing mattered. If it didn't matter, why'd she keep on? It hadn't bothered him at first, but the more she told him it was okay, the more he thought it wasn't. And this on top of everything else.

There was a swishing sound of cloth on floor and he looked over to see Dandy crawling into the room. He bumped into the wall before he got turned around toward the bed. He pulled into the bottom corner and sat there, making a lot of nonsense sounds and waving his arms around. After a time he stretched out onto his stomach and went to sleep. Jolene never stopped working on Artie. He felt uncomfortable about that, having the kid see his mother that way. He didn't know how to explain it to her, though.

"He called me Dada the other day," Artie said. He didn't know why he told her that. It struck him now as the saddest thing he'd ever heard, and one loud sob burst from his mouth before he got control of himself. Jolene moved up and rubbed his face. "We got to get out of this shit and get out of it fast," he said. He looked at Dandy, at Jolene, at the ceiling, then the window. "There's troubles and then there's troubles," he told her. "We got troubles."

"Honey, any way I can help, anything you think of, just tell me. I owe you," she said; then, softer, "I wish I never got that damn letter."

He thought about it all: the fight, the whore, the rings, Jolene. He thought about the Jell-O wrestling and the move in and how everything was going fine until that Gristel guy stepped in. He thought about that. Then he thought about the car breaking down and the argument and the driver who picked up Jolene. Artie remembered smacking his hand on the car window, watching them disappear up the bridge into the storm. He thought about Gristel. He thought about the driver and Jolene together. Jolene told him the guy said he'd be back; she thought tomorrow, but she wasn't sure. He thought about the other guy in the car, and about Gristel and the unit—the TV, stereo, recliner, washing machine . . . all those things he'd never have in his life unless things changed real fast. Paintings on the wall—he wasn't big on paintings, but it'd be something if he was able to put one up, if he had the option.

He thought about the unit again, and about Gristel selling just a little piece of time for other people to use. But they didn't really own it. He saw that now. Gristel, he guessed, still owned it. All the other people had was a little piece of it. Gristel was the guy who ran the show. The guy who said "when." The guy who called the shots. The man everybody respected.

He looked down at Jolene and ran his thumbs over his fingers as if feeling paper money. There was a deep root of sadness, a cramping pain, twisting through his stomach. I ain't going to deal with that, he told himself. He found he couldn't look at Jolene without feeling like he was going to cry. He'd had enough of that to last a lifetime. He moved to that other part of his brain, the part that wanted to make her pay for what she'd done to him.

It'll just be temporary, he told himself. Only for a short while. Just until they got up a stake. They were both grown up; they could handle it. It wasn't really anything. Nothing that would make any difference for them. There was all that other time, too. The days and weeks and months and years that'd be theirs.

"What are you thinking about, honey?" she asked.

He pulled the blanket over his head to kill the coldness shaking through him. "Time sharing," he said. "It's the only way."

# CHAPTER
# —19—

He sat on the stairs near the landing above her apartment and waited. The gunhole window at his back bent his shadow down a half a dozen steps in a staggered, thinning line. In the light around his shadow, a dense mist of dust hung in constant suspension.

He was turned toward his left, his face pressed between the square posts of two railings. The damp odor of rot mixed with the oily smell of paint and irritated his nostrils. But he didn't move, just sat there watching Jolene's door.

He'd been there since noon, staring down the stairwell at the darkness, which thickened as it got closer to the ground floor. Every ten minutes Jolene stepped into the hall. She'd show him a smile meant to be cheerful, but her mouth was shaky at the corners and she couldn't hide the deep trenches of sadness beneath her eyes. Sometimes she'd wave. Sometimes she'd bring Dandy out, haul him on her arm, and wave his arm for him. Artie was sure the kid never saw him, never picked out his face from between the bars. It was probably for the best.

She'd cried a lot when he first brought it up. But it hadn't been too hard to convince her. By the morning the crying had become a steady whimper. "What choice do we have?" he asked. Of course she couldn't come up with nothing to say. The answer was clear. They didn't even have a second pick. "It's this or nothing. And it's not like he's a stranger. It didn't seem to bother you when you were doing it for yourself. Least you can do is do it for me. For us. To help me out, us out. To help your own kid." He found himself hating her and wanting her to be hurt, maybe even murdered. But when he left to sit on the stairs he felt different. Watching her, feeling apart from her and looking down at it all, he thought maybe he'd made a big mistake. How could he tell her that, though? How could he admit he was wrong? And where else was the money going to come from?

Being up there on the stairs, he felt there was something of himself he'd left behind in that apartment. He couldn't figure what.

He began to hope the man would never show up. The hours passed and he held that wish in the front of his mind. Jolene continued stepping out, smiling and waving, and Artie pretended it was all some game they were playing. He sat patiently, showing her no emotion. It surprised him, that he could be so still. He'd never done that before. He figured it had to do with his head. His head felt like it'd been hollowed out from inside, as if something had exploded in there and destroyed the core of his brain, leaving only a thin shell of skullbone. There was a tight, wound quality to his muscles. That scared him. It felt like if his body shifted into motion he wouldn't be able to stop it.

"It's almost dark," Jolene called. "I'm sure he would've come by now." She twisted her hands back and forth on the top curved bar of the railing. She pointed her face up at him. "Please, Artie. Come down, honey. Let's let it be over."

He stood and stretched. He wasn't sure about quitting. How else was he going to take care of her? It was a man's responsibility to see his woman was taken care of. As he stood, though, relief curled up from his feet through his legs, torso, arms, and fingers. He held the railing with one hand, smiled, and said, "Well, gal—"

The outside door opened with a low creak.

They both peered down and ducked back quickly as the man looked up. They could tell from his clothing he didn't live there. Who else could he be?

A whirl of faintness gripped him. Artie dropped to a sitting position. White dots whizzed like atoms before his eyes. "Artie," Jolene whispered, her voice like air escaping from a balloon.

"Honey." The footsteps pounded closer. Steady, deliberate. "Please," she said, the word a short burst.

He couldn't look at her. He sat in a cloud as the footsteps thudded louder, then stopped. A man's voice, full of laughter, said, "Waiting eagerly, I see."

The door slammed shut and Artie was on his feet, down the stairs; one flight, two, three. He slipped on the last three steps and landed on his ass in the foyer. He jumped up and thrust open the outer door. He shoved it so hard it banged against the brick building front and the large single-pane window shattered. Across the street, he looked back. The light in their room flickered on and she came to the window. She looked down at him and raised her hand to wave or make some motion. He turned and headed up the street.

Within half a block he stopped. The car, he told himself. Get the car. The big black Cadillac. It had to be nearby. A car like that you couldn't hide. He looked around and realized the Cadillac was Gristel's car. He couldn't remember what this guy's was like. Something small. He stood on the sidewalk, staring up and down the street, and it shocked him to notice the snow had all melted. A few of the yards in front of the apartment buildings were fenced in, and behind these fences the trees were in bud. There wasn't even any fog coming out of his mouth. What did it matter, though? He wanted to smash and break and slash things. His nails dug into the palms of his clenched fists. A side mirror on the car to his right showed Artie a patch of his face, half a chin, the side of his mouth. He kicked his boot up and knocked the mirror to the ground. It clattered on the sidewalk without breaking.

He concentrated harder, trying to fill the space where his mind should be, but the harder he tried to focus, the more removed he felt from himself. He turned back to the apartment. The light snapped off. A gaffing hook of sorrow punctured him from behind, drove through his chest, and jerked him backward. The street rolled away; a slamming pain shot through his back; he reached out his hands and discovered he was sprawled on the sidewalk. Above him the solid gray mass of sky looked as heavy as a plaster mold of mountains. He thought of Jolene, how long it would take her to make the money, how many weeks and months. Dandy'd be in there the whole time, watching, and Artie'd have to sit out here, just like this, looking up at something pressing down on him, something he could never reach. All the time knowing she was in there with someone else. It was too much. It was just too much. It felt like someone had played all his options on him without giving him any choice, any say in his situation. This was it. Enough was enough. He wasn't going to let them do it to him. Not this time. Not anymore. He'd show them. His rage built, settled inside his chest, all tense and ready to spring. "What the hell you doing on the ground?" he said to himself. He stood up. The time had come for action.

The door fronting the alley was hanging from its bottom hinge and slanted open against the inner wall. Artie walked past it, up the stairs. Halfway up a new, large gouge of plaster had been torn or smashed from the pale green wall, leaving a hole looking into darkness. He stopped before it. The magic spot, he thought. The place for answers. He peered into the blackness and waited to feel forces, vibrations, anything. Its deadness seemed to charge the energy in his limbs. A shooting force surged through his fingers. He punched the edge of the hole with the side of his fist. Plaster cracked, but none caved in.

He rapped once, hard, on the door. George opened it a crack, the gold line of the chain lock a thin mask for her eyes. A smile slithered, lizardlike, across her mouth. She shut the door to remove the chain. When she reopened it she posed with one leg forward, one hand on the door, the other on the doorframe. She was wearing a faded blue negligee. "Well, look what the cat dragged in," she said. "Or should I say, look what the cat tossed out?"

"Don't give me no hassles," Artie said. "Anyone gives me hassles from here on in, they're going to be sorry." He rocked on his heels and tried to look important.

"Manners," George said. "I could've told you she wasn't your type. She looked like she belonged on Championship Wrestling. The shoulders on her, my God. She was a woman?"

"Look, I ain't in the mood, George, all right? I'm warning you once." He shifted from foot to foot, hesitated, then pushed her arm off the doorframe and stepped inside.

"Well," George said huffily. She turned and shut the door, then set her hands on her hips and pushed her left shoulder forward.

The room was brightly lit by the overhead coil. Just to the right of the entrance, atop the refrigerator, were the hot plate and toaster. Beyond that the porcelain sink. A medicine cabinet mirror had been hung sideways above the sink, and it reflected the splotchy rust-colored stain around the drain below.

"Who do you think you are?" George said. "Pushing me around. I have a good mind to tell Denny." She folded her arms and rubbed her shoulders. "He's been looking for you, Sweets, did you know that? Denny and that other man. The fat one? Smitty? He's mad enough to kill. I'm sure they'd take care of me if I told them you were here. Why shouldn't I?"

Artie was pacing the room. His foot caught, as if he were stumbling, but he forced it forward. "Shut up, just shut up. I thought you were my friend." He spun around and made a cutting motion with his hand in the air above his head. "I've had it up to here." He wiped his hands down his face, blew out a breath, then sat on the bed. The electric heater, plugged in beside the sink, made a rattling hum. He looked at the red zigzags of the heating element and felt like kicking it over. He couldn't think and he didn't even want to talk to anybody, but he had to do both. In his mind he pictured himself taking the guy with the knife, throwing him to the ground, lifting the black girl off Jolene with one hand. Then him and Jolene would hop into a Cadillac and be driven off somewhere, for happy carefree times.

"What are you talking about, Sweets?" George put a hand onto each cheek and split her lips slightly open, then went to the mirror over the sink and adjusted her expression. It took awhile to find the right attitude of surprise and concern.

Beside the bed was a night table. A tube of lipstick lay before a round makeup mirror. Artie pocketed the lipstick. Present for Jolene. The mirror was the two-sided kind, and he flipped it to the magnifying side. His nose was a swollen growth, covered by pores clogged with grease and dirt. The rough growth of hair on his cheeks and chin made him think of jungles and machetes. When he opened his mouth his teeth appeared as dangerous sharp crags and peaks, occasional black tunnels.

He angled the mirror to catch his narrow, bloodshot eyes. They seemed on the verge of popping from their sockets. They wouldn't stay still. He thought his face looked threatening, the face of a man capable of anything. A face people would listen to. A face people would obey. That was almost like respect, he thought. He studied himself and his heart gave a quick shudder. It didn't look like him, in the mirror there. It looked like a different person. Not better, just different. He spun the mirror back. Something snapped inside him. It seemed to bounce along the walls of a deep well. He touched the table, the bed, himself. Felt them all. But it wasn't quite like making contact.

George sat beside him, shifted close, and rubbed Artie's knee.

Artie stood up to explain something. He opened his mouth, but a hot block of air walled in his words. He shook his head. From his pocket he pulled out the money—Jolene's money. She'd given it to him along with her confession. Two twenties, one ten, seven ones. He rolled the bills into a tube, which seemed so small as to be insubstantial.

George widened her eyes, surprised and flattered. She glanced at herself in the full-length mirror on the metal wardrobe across from the foot of the bed. She fluttered her negligee once and looked at Artie. "*You* want to *buy* some action?"

"I want the gun."

She seemed confused at first, then insulted. "Oh, that's it? Well, it's not for sale."

"I want to rent it: one day." He unrolled the bills and fanned them out, feeling the cool dryness of the paper, the slipperiness.

She arched her neck to look at the money. "Sweets, now—"

"Don't Sweets-now me. I know what I'm doing." He became

aware of the sweat on his face and wiped his jacket sleeve across his forehead. "Don't try to tell me what to do, what's good for me." The heater sounded like it was gargling metal coins. He spun, bent, snapped it off, shook his finger at George. "I'm thirty-seven years old," he said. He dropped the bills in her lap. "Thirty-seven. Remember that."

George counted the money, then pulled up her negligee. On her right thigh she wore a black lace garter, a red band in the middle. There was a holster made from a dungaree pocket on the inside, with a sewed-on snap that held an American Derringer in place. She removed the gun and passed it to Artie. "One day," she said. "How do I know you'll return it?"

He felt the small weight as he hefted the gun, the comfortable way it fit, like a key for doors he'd never been able to open. There were possibilities here, he thought.

"It's not like it's real," George said. "I mean, of course it's 'real.' But you can't expect much from something that size. It's all talk, if you know what I mean."

Something popped behind his eyes. Dizziness tore through him, flashing from one side of his head to the other. He poked the gun into George's face. It hit her nose and she jerked back; then Artie was atop her, straddling her legs, the barrel dug into the cheek beneath her left eye. "It's big enough to blow your fucking head off," he said. "It's big enough to get the fucking job done. Man, I'm sick of this shit."

George whimpered and Artie pushed off her and stood up. He walked to the mirror at the foot of the bed.

"You're sick all right," George said, sitting up and making mending motions on her face with her fingers. "You've lost it, honey."

Artie looked at himself in the mirror: a thin, wasted man with a gun barely visible in his hand. He was stunned at how drawn he looked, like a man at the end of a long illness that was eating him up. He didn't want to see any more, and he hustled out the door. As he passed the hole he slowed, stopped a few steps below it, turned, and went back. He remembered the look on George's face when he pushed the gun at her. She'd been afraid of him for a few seconds, and he felt good about that. He'd been in control. He slid the lipstick tube from his pocket and tossed the top onto the steps. It rolled and rattled softly down a few stairs. THIS IS WEAR I LIVE, he wrote. He stopped to think. BOY ARE YOU GOIN A BE SORRIE. He dropped the lipstick and hurried out.

He spit on the glass door, kicked it with the bottom of his foot. A uniformed attendant came out and yelled at him. "Hey, get out of here or we're calling the cops."

"Call yourself a bus station?" Artie yelled over his shoulder as he walked away. "Don't even know where Sunbelt is."

The attendant shook his head and went back inside. The hell with them, Artie thought. He'd wanted some idea of what the tickets would cost, so he'd know how much he had to get. But the idiots in there: "I don't think it's a town, I think it's an area." How could you buy a ticket to an area? Well, it was their loss. He'd go to a real bus station, someplace where they knew what was what. Or maybe they'd fly. Or buy a car.

He crossed the street toward a skyscraper like a giant silver H, with strip windows the color of fish tanks across the building's front. There was an attached building, the same glowing silver color, but it had no windows. He thought maybe there weren't any real people in there. He imagined robots, with antennae and insect eyes. They'd be working on conveyor belts—*they'd* be putting together the people. Maybe sometimes they'd twist one part around, or take out a little piece of the brain. Something. One slight change to screw up the works. "All my goddamn life," Artie said, and he realized he was talking to himself. He looked around for someone to direct his remarks to and found a young girl with spiky platinum hair, wearing a black Spandex jumpsuit and red leather jacket, sitting on the grass in front of the windowless building. She was smoking a joint. "All my life," he told the girl, "I go to put my feet forward and they go off to the sides somewheres."

"You got a problem," the girl said, standing up.

"Yeah, yeah, I got a problem all right. I got a problem, sweetheart." He felt the gun in his pocket and sneered. "And I got a solution right here." It might not be the right solution, he thought. But it was the one he had.

"You're a fucking creep." The girl snorted and walked away before he could even tell her off.

He went on, pushed to speed by his rage, thinking he should've pulled out the gun and shot her in the foot, taught her a lesson. He'd show them, he thought. He'd show all of them they couldn't screw around with him no more. He followed alongside the raised expressway, the outer walls a dead green strip. The exhaust from the rush-hour traffic formed a thick sooty cloud over the roadway, obscuring the squares and blocks of the buildings behind it. Horns coughed and blared in rapid streams, like sudden arguments. As he walked, his confidence flaked off bit by bit.

He passed the bridges leading to the docks on his right, then the Aquarium, set back from the road, its flags snapping in the breeze. A large orange metal sculpture dove and surfaced like a whale in the darkening, overcast sky. Lights were coming on in all the buildings around him, yellow and cream squares. His movement was slower, his legs shaky and heavy. He wanted to run, to go back to the apartment, but he thought of Jolene, and the man, and clung to the small, encapsulated growth of his purpose. He wanted to do one thing right. He wanted to get them out of this mess. Down to Sunbelt, or wherever a man could find opportunity. He wanted to show people he could make it.

He veered into the park at the waterfront, past the new hotel that reminded him of a brick pyramid. Caravans of black clouds ran the rim of the harbor, north to south. He could make out the airport by the runway lights, and he watched a jet take off, rise until its red lights dwindled from sight. In the summer the water would be full of jellyfish pushed and tossed by the dark chop of waves. He stared at the empty water and told himself, You do it now or it's over for you. He released his mind to thoughts of Jolene, then, something he'd been trying not to do. He was overwhelmed with their intensity. He thought about his love for her, and how he wanted her to love him in return and to be proud. A blade of anguish sliced through his lungs.

He stopped at the corner of the cement warehouse, which had been sandblasted on the outside so the exterior would be suitable for the exclusive shops and realtors' offices that filled the white-walled track-lit interior. He was waiting for Store 24 in the front of the building to be less crowded. He'd picked the place because it was near his old neighborhood, and he figured he'd be able to run out and hide someplace pretty easily. The register was right near the door, too, so it wouldn't take him long.

He waited for a long time. People were going in, coming out, going in. It never stopped. The harbor was a gray slit at the rear of the building, and he pretended to be absorbed in it any time someone stared at him. He leaned on the blue mailbox on the corner, hoping to receive some sign. As he waited he let his fingers soothe the gun in his pocket.

He tried to sing snatches of songs, any song. But the music was gone from his mind. He was having trouble with his voice, too, and once it even felt like there were fingers on his throat. He finally decided the hell with it. People or no people, it didn't matter. He couldn't wait any longer. People were always in his way. Why should this time be any different?

He looked through the glass window as he walked toward the door. A boy slouched on the stool behind the register and rang up orders. A young kid, with short blond hair. For a brief, startling instant the boy's hair seemed to be some alien growth eating its way through the back of his skull. Artie's legs trembled, bent him lower, threatened to make him tumble to the ground. His left hand shook so much he had to use his right one, too, to open the door with. In that second, when he lost contact with the gun, his entire self shriveled into a fist-sized stone centered just below his heart. "Jolene darling," he said to himself. He wrapped his fingers quickly around the gun again. The core expanded, spread back through his system. He had the sense that with each inhale his body was inflating, adding one more layer of bulk, and he breathed hungrily. But on each exhale his heart beat so loud he thought it would shake the store and tumble the cans and boxes from the shelves. He stood just inside the door, incapable of movement, trapped between the need to breathe and the terror of the release. His mouth was dry, coppery tasting. He could feel the vibrations of a voice inside him, a voice of warning and rationale, beginning to insinuate itself into his consciousness, maybe offer him a way out. He knew if he could just have one minute of peace, to wait for the voice to come through, it would be revealed to him what was required in his life. He was unable to move without those directions. He felt something shaping up inside his head, saw a mouth opening to give the word, and just as he was on the verge of receiving its message, a woman clutching a small brown sack said, "Excuse me," and passed by him out the door.

Artie moved his free hand up to clutch at his forehead. Everything inside rolled away. He had a sense of dark wells, whirlpools, descending through his system.

"Looking for something?" the boy behind the register called out to him.

"Yeah," Artie heard a voice say. "Yeah, I'm looking for something. I just don't know what." The voice seemed to come from his mouth. His limbs tingled, felt solid again. No one was in front of the register, though several heads poked above the aisles. Artie was moving forward, words oozing from his mouth without his having any awareness of what he was saying. The aisles to his right took on a festive demeanor. Bright colors and shapes surrounded him just beyond his ability to define them. It seemed like a party. He heard a voice say, "I ain't garbage," as he stepped before the register, his head just above the lower edge of the counter. He looked at the boy, who was wearing a red pin-striped shirt and leather tie. He leaned over Artie. On the counter to his left, a lottery machine's small periscope was raised higher than Artie's face. It was looking down at him.

On the count of two he pulled the gun from his pocket. It stuck for a second and he started to panic; then it came free. Artie flashed the Derringer and a smile at the same time. He told the boy, "Give me everything you're worth."

"Is this a joke, sir?" The boy looked at the gun. "That's a toy, right?"

"I ain't a joke!" Artie yelled.

There were shuffling sounds at his back, people moving closer. Sweat oozed around his eyebrows and into his eyes from both sides. He tried to squint and blink away the salty blur. His arms were shaking. The gun barrel bobbed as he held it in his clenched hands. Everything was moving, spinning in a half circle one way, then coming back in the other direction. In the center of it all, the only stable thing, was the boy's face. "I come in here like an honest man," Artie said. He held the gun at the extent of his arms, pointed up, but he couldn't stop it from shaking.

Behind him someone laughed. The boy smiled. A woman's voice said, "Just a drunk." Maybe he could get out of this, Artie thought. Maybe he could walk away. Maybe he could put the gun in his pocket and say, I was just kidding. But then where would he be? What about Jolene? What would they think of him? He wanted to sit down and figure it all out. Say "Freeze" and have the whole place frozen in this moment while he thought. But before he could start, before he could come up with the first word to say, there was a quick rushing sound at his back, feet hitting the floor like fists slamming a speed bag, and he was bumped from behind. Arms groped around his sides, hands flayed at his wrists, and he crashed forward, a weight on his back. His arms hit the counter and the gun went off.

There was silence; then someone screamed, the sound like a gull screeching overhead. Hands released him, the weight pulled off, and he had a sudden impulse to say, Don't let go of me. He pushed himself away from the rack of LifeSavers and gum. He expected to see the boy shattered, but when he looked up he was whole. A small bloom of blood was growing on the boy's shirt just above his belt, but he hadn't moved. His face fell open now and he touched his hands to the bloody spot as if covering up exposed privates. He took two tentative steps backward and sat heavily on the floor, out of sight.

Artie shook. He couldn't put himself, the gun, and the boy together. He'd seen things on TV a few times, but this was like none of that. It was so quiet. The first shock hit his legs with an unstoppable jittering. He held onto the counter, so he wouldn't fall, and tried to throw the gun off. But it was fused to his hands. His fingers wouldn't bend open. He couldn't let go.

He stumbled out the door like a man with palsy. He expected to see the violent motions of undefined forces, buildings and streets, heaving upward and twisting into warped configurations. When he looked back over his shoulder, nothing had changed. All was calm. Maybe nothing had really happened after all, he thought. Maybe none of this was real. But as he stared at Store 24, moving figures streamed out the door, pointed at him, and rushed to the phone booths lining the sidewalk across the street.

He trudged into the gloom under the expressway. The thumping roll of cars and trucks passed overhead. The green girders, mangy with rust, gave off slight tremors. He looked at the rivets, half the size of his fist, and imagined them shooting straight out through his forehead.

"Oh, Jolene . . ." he said. He slouched against a cement abutment surrounding a support post. Above him the expressway shuddered. The scent of blood and the buzz of flies came vividly to his senses, and he looked at his hand, the gun—so small. "Jolene," he said again. He began talking to her, saying her name, trying to arrange other words to follow. But the only comprehensible sound he could make was "Jolene."

He sat mumbling, making guttural sounds, feeling the press of an enormous sorrow on the inside of his chest. It was a sorrow having to do with the boy, but more with Jolene and himself, even Dandy; a sorrow for what he knew he'd be missing. He imagined blood spurting from his hair, the gush so heavy he'd soon be stained with red. It would drip from his hands, run off his clothing, cover the cement, and pour into the street. Cars speeding by would splash it back on him. He was sweating all over and he could hardly breathe. Fear sheeted down his face, up the back of his head, and down his face again in a continuous, racing motion. Everywhere he turned he saw the boy, as if the image projected from his forehead. On the passing cars, the cement divider, the girders overhead—he saw the blood bloom. A pigeon floated to a halt near his feet. "I did it," Artie said. The pigeon cocked its head. He said it again, but he wasn't sure the words made it outside his mouth. The pigeon took a few pecking swipes, then flapped off.

"Jolene!" he cried, the word carrying through the air. It echoed back from the underside of the steel overpass. Then he heard the siren in the distance, a solid keening, moving closer. He wondered what he could possibly tell them. What could he say? Where were the words to explain all this?

He looked at his legs stretched flat before him, at the gun set in his hand in his lap. It took up all his vision, and unconsciously he began to rock. "I'm a man of some means," he said, nodding to himself and pursing his lips. The siren was so close it hurt his ears. He shook his head and stared at the silver barrel. "Everybody knows Artie."

# CHAPTER
# —20—

Jolene went out to buy food, and also because she was afraid. It was already dark and he wasn't back. It was his idea and he wasn't back. Was he just going to leave them like this? She had a feeling that something bad, something really bad had happened to him. No, it couldn't have, she told herself. He knew how to take care of himself. She was just getting herself all worked up over nothing. If she was out of the house, he'd come back. Watched water doesn't boil. She'd just go out and pick up a few things and he'd be there when she returned. Nothing could happen to him. He was Artie.

She shopped at the small grocery store two blocks away. She bought lettuce, tomatoes, French dressing, a bottle of Cold Duck, and a real steak from the meat counter for him. At the register she picked up a *TV Guide*. "The best-selling magazine in America," the display said. She added it to her purchases. There must be something to it, if everybody was buying it. So what if they didn't own a TV yet. It was good to have things around the house for Dandy to look at, books and stuff. Maybe he'd even teach himself how to read. They could always get a TV, if the money kept coming in. A TV and a radio with real speakers. And some clothes and shoes. Cigarettes. And curtains. Blankets, a couch, some army men for Dandy. She thought about all the things they could buy, but it didn't help her. It didn't make her feel any better.

Then she thought about Dandy's eyes. Why'd he have to have that problem? It'd take a year at this rate to save up enough money for that. How were they ever going to make enough to get out of this? She saw her life stretched before her like a skid mark on tar—going on and on and just ending, never having gone anywhere.

"Nine dollars and forty-six cents, ma'am," the girl behind the register said. Jolene handed her a ten. She guessed the girl to be her own age, but she looked so young. Her skin was smooth and her hair was fluffy, her eyes bright. Jolene stared at her own reflection in the window at the front of the store, the dark gouges under her eyes, the sagging of her cheeks, her limp hair, the way her shoulders slumped in toward her chest.

On the sidewalk before the store a folding table was set up. A severe, angry woman dressed in military fatigues sat there holding some sort of petition in her hand. She waved Jolene over and explained what it was all about. Jolene was still thinking about Artie, though, and she only half heard. What came through didn't seem to make a lot of sense. Something to do with "rights." She couldn't quite make it out. There were a lot of political-type words: dominance, structures, equality. The woman was talking about problems and solutions but there weren't any examples. She didn't seem to be talking about any sort of real things that ever came along in Jolene's life. It was just words, problems with words.

"Never mind 'sexist,'" Jolene said. "How can I pay for my baby's eyes?"

"This is a global struggle," the woman said. "You have to look beyond your own personal problems. We're talking international solidarity." She held the petition forward for Jolene to sign.

"I got nothing to do with that. None of that don't touch my life," Jolene said.

"Don't be stupid," the woman told her.

Jolene couldn't use none of that in her life right now, and she turned around. The woman called out after her, but Jolene tuned her out. It was just so much noise coming from the woman's mouth, not much different than the cars making their noise as they passed by on the street. She didn't have time for "rights" in her life; maybe that was the problem. One of them. But she just didn't have time. You just *do,* she thought. Her life was ticking on and she had enough trouble just trying to keep up with it, let alone think about it.

"I'm home, honey," she called, but the words dispersed in the air. She put the groceries away. "Artie?" she called. The bathroom was empty. In the bedroom Dandy slept stretched where the man had been. She tossed the *TV Guide* to the mattress, then hung her coat in the closet. She looked at the pileup of dogs, the stuffed dog's head atop it. The man had seen that on the floor and picked it up. "Is this your baby's?" he'd asked, smirking.

"That's right," she told him, and she took it from him and put it safely away in the closet.

Now she spread the ceramic dogs out onto the floor around her. She searched through them, noticing for the first time that a number of them were cracked, broken. She must've done that, she thought, and she felt like crying. She set those aside, put them back in the closet, thinking to get some glue, find some pieces to fix them with, and surprise Artie. The good ones she lined up on the floor in front of her.

Taking a few in her hands at a time, she traveled around the house and set them in windows. She put them in the corners of the rooms, and two behind the toilet. She put one on the steak in the refrigerator, and another beside the bottle of Cold Duck. It excited her and she hurried to finish, talking to Artie as she worked. "Please honey give me one more minute, just one more minute." He'd be so surprised. He'd be thrilled. It would make it more like a home for him.

She snapped off the kitchen light and sat at the table, waiting, ready to yell "Surprise!" Cars drove by outside and people moved through the building, coming in, going out. Doors opened, closed, and she jumped at every one. But none of them were for her. She moved her hands across the table, staring at her fingers, ghostly in the distant cast from the streetlight. She bent forward until she was slumped on the table, her stomach feeding on itself. Finally she couldn't stand it anymore, the being alone with herself.

She went to the bedroom, shucked her clothes off, lifted Dandy from the bed, and draped a blanket around her shoulders. He was a heavy pull on her arm as she moved to the side of the stove. He started to shift into consciousness, and she sat down quickly, trying to settle him. The floor was warm and she faced the flames, holding him in her lap. She ran her tongue around her mouth, tasting the thick, musky flavor of the man. She wanted that to make her nauseous, make her hate herself, make her feel something. But it was just one more detail in her life. She felt she was already used to it, and that made her bitter.

Dandy grunted and squirmed. He wanted to leave, to get to the floor. "Will you just please stay still?" she said, her voice squealing. He kept moving. "Dandy!" He rolled and pushed at her hands, then started whining. "Okay then, get off," she yelled, and pushed him so hard he flew from her lap. His face smacked the grill by the gas log and he fell to the floor, screaming.

"Oh my God my baby!" Jolene cried. She gathered him to her quickly. The left earpiece of his glasses was broken, and there were three burn stripes on his left cheek. She kissed him all over the face. "I'm sorry I'm sorry I'm sorry I'm sorry I'm sorry," she told him. "Oh, baby." It took him a long time to calm down. Dear God, what is going to happen to us? she thought. "Honey, I didn't mean it. Mama's got a lot of pressure right now, please be nice to her."

She wrapped the blanket tightly around the both of them, fixing it so only their heads stuck out. The blue flames flickered behind the barred grill. Striped shadows bound her legs where they stretched out of the blanket. She pretended they were in a big house, before a marble fireplace loaded with logs. They'd be waiting, just waiting, for something grand and wonderful to happen. Something just great. "Something like . . ." she said. She thought about it a long time. The room pulled close in the darkness. Something that she didn't even know how to wish for.